The Quest

Audrey Harrison

Published by Audrey Harrison

Find more about the author and contact details at the end of this book and the chance to obtain a free copy of The Unwilling Earl.

Proofread and edited by Jenny Warren and can be contacted at jenny@warrenproofreading.co.uk or www.warrenproofreading.co.uk

Cover by Covers and Cupcakes
www.coversandcupcakes.com

Chapter 1

London 1815

"Let me go, you damned cur!" The voice rang out through the darkened alleyway. As the captive was wriggling and kicking like some trapped wild animal, it was no surprise that she was soon released and fell to the ground with a painful sounding 'ooff'.

"You were being followed, you foolish chit," the stranger growled out, knowing that his ribs would have bruises for days after the battering he had just received from her elbows.

"It was all under control," came the ungrateful reply.

"So much so that you could not escape my grasp until I released you. Tell me, how were you intending to fight three of them off?"

"I had a plan." It was clearly a lie, but was said with furious vehemence.

Hugh Weston, Earl of Bryn, laughed with genuine amusement, something those who knew him would find astonishing. The Earl of Bryn did not bark out a laugh; he sneered, snubbed and looked derisively through his quizzing glass. It was a fine day indeed if he smiled. But laughed? Never!

"This I have to hear. Tell me more, I beg of you," he said, his disbelieving tone expressing fully his feelings about the comment.

"I would love to pass the time of day with you, but some of us have work to do," came the dismissive reply.

Before Hugh could respond, she had jumped to her feet, turned on her heel and ran. Her movements were fast and without a sound across the rough pavements of the less salubrious streets of London.

For a moment, Hugh considered chasing her, but he knew when he was on a fool's errand. Within seconds she had disappeared from sight, and with her black clothing she would soon blend into the dark night.

It had been pure chance he had seen her, and more importantly, the men who were clearly following her. At least they had disappeared the moment he had made his move to act the rescuer; if they had chosen that moment to attack, they would have had two for the price of one, so to speak, for the wriggling fish he had tried to hold meant he could not have protected them both.

He had recognised her gait as that of a female, even though she was dressed in male attire and wearing a large masquerade mask. One who was a keen observer of people had been quick to pick up on the unconscious signs she had betrayed. If her pursuers had caught her, she would have had a fate not worth dwelling on, for it would remind him how precarious life was on these streets, and for his own reasons, he could not acknowledge thoughts like that.

Picking up his cane from where he had abandoned it, he straightened his hat, brushed his frock coat down and walked into the night, in the opposite direction from which the young woman had run. She was on her own now, the foolish chit. It would have interrupted his own activities, but he was gentleman enough that he would have seen her to safety if she had remained with him. There was nothing more he could do for her; sometimes, one had to accept that you could not help those who did not want it, and she was clearly foolhardy in the extreme. He would probably read of her murder in tomorrow's paper, for he was certain she could not protect herself, no matter how much she protested otherwise.

His frown did not mar his features as he thought about holding her, it was after all a usual expression for Hugh, but there had been something hard around her body when he had grasped her. It was as if she was wearing some sort of armour underneath her clothes. It was strange and had surprised him a little, hence she had been able to inflict far more injury on him than she normally would have achieved. He would regret his momentary lapse in concentration every time one of the bruises twinged.

As he walked, he could not dismiss the encounter as easily as he would have liked. What was her business? Her accent was not that of the usual people who lived and worked in the area, but then again, neither was his.

His lips tilted in a half-smile as he contemplated the looks of horror he would receive from his acquaintances if they knew where he was. Thankfully, he did not give a damn what anyone else thought; he had a job to do, and he had made a promise to himself. If it took him years, he would complete his task and right a wrong that haunted him.

Turning a corner, he nodded to his coach driver and the two footmen who accompanied his trips into the underbelly of the great city. They were fully armed and willing to guard the carriage, but when he went out, he went alone. Staying with the carriage, they were reasonably safe; he would not put them at risk amongst the people he had to speak to. That was his duty alone, and although he took precautions, he would not put anyone else in harm's way, especially those who were in no position to object.

Leaning back as the carriage moved away from the squalor, he sighed, no results tonight. Again.

Crossing his ankles, he grimaced at the state of his boots, visible in the lit carriage. His valet was going to sulk for days at the scuffs on the fine leather. It seemed as if the chit had kicked half of London's dirty streets onto his boots as she fought to escape. He could almost hear the peal his valet would ring over him, as any servant who had been in their master's employ since he was a young boy felt they could do.

Hugh turned and looked blindly out of the window. For once, his thoughts were not about the next stages of his search; the woman in black filled his mind. Who was she, and what was she doing in such a dangerous place?

***

Julia leaned against the inside wall of the servant's entrance to her home, breathing heavily to try to slow her pounding heart. She had run further than she had ever done before and faster and was feeling the effects of it. How had she been caught so easily? She cursed to herself as she tilted her head back in an effort to get as much air in her lungs as possible.

What had she been thinking? The last anniversary of her parents' death had hit her hard. She had no idea why, whether it was to do with the past or the future, but whatever had caused it, she had come to a decision. She could not let others suffer the same fate as her parents.

Coming up with the scheme to patrol the streets at night and intervene if she saw anything amiss had seemed a good idea when she had been seated in a comfortable drawing room in broad daylight. Not so much when she was alone at night.

She could have stopped after the first night, but the need to do something was there, even though she was afraid. She had never done anything so outrageous in her life before, and whenever she returned home, safe, there was an overwhelming sense of relief. Refusing to let the fear control her, she determined to continue on her quest, though it would shock everyone who knew her.

Finally able to breathe normally, she forced herself off the wall and prepared to go up to her chamber.

"Is that you, Julia?" came the quiet voice of her uncle down the servant's stairs.

"Yes, it is I," she replied, trying to make her voice sound normal. "I will be up shortly." Taking off her boots, which had been adapted to make less noise underfoot, she started the climb up to her uncle. Resigned to telling him what had gone on, she set her shoulders; he would be worried and concerned, but it would not alter anything. She was determined to keep helping those at risk in any way she could.

"Oh Julia, that was too close a call," Uncle William said after Julia had explained about being followed and then taken by surprise. "I know I am no longer your guardian, but I hope I hold some sway over you, and I beg of you to stop this crusade you have embarked on."

"Uncle, you know I cannot," Julia said, trying to make him understand, but feeling compassion for him, for she knew he worried. "Tonight, those men were going to attack a couple who were just walking through the streets after an evening out. They had done nothing wrong and did not deserve to be robbed, or worse." It was the same discussion they had shared every few days since she had started her night-time ventures.

"No one does, but it is not your responsibility to protect anyone foolish enough not to hire a carriage in the dead of night," Uncle William counterargued.

"Are you saying we should not walk the streets after dark? You know that is not the answer. These people who are preying on the innocent need to be stopped," Julia responded.

"I agree that they do, and that is why we have Bow Street Runners."

"Pfftt," Julia huffed. "I have never seen a single one on the streets at night; they are no use. You know the finest areas can employ someone to keep the peace, so there is less of a problem there, but that still leaves too many streets unprotected."

"You are too vulnerable."

Julia smiled at him. "I have your inventions to protect me."

"Much good they did you tonight."

"Yes, it shows I need something else in addition to the pepper solution you gave me. It proved great in the trials we did, but needing two hands to use it is clearly a disadvantage in practice."

"I wish you would carry a gun."

"No. I will not kill anyone. If I carry a gun, I risk an innocent person being killed for just being in the wrong place at the wrong time."

William reached across and squeezed Julia's hand. "It was such a long time ago now. Is it not time to let them rest in peace?"

"It might be twelve years ago, but nothing has changed; innocent people are still being hurt," Julia answered, tears making her eyes sparkle. It did not matter how much time had passed; it still hurt to have lost her parents in such a sudden and brutal way.

"I miss them too," William said gently. "But they would hate to know that you put yourself in danger night after night."

"I take as many precautions as my uncle can invent." Julia grinned, trying to lighten the mood and deflect her uncle from the lecture about giving up her activities. She understood why he said that her parents would not be happy with what she was doing, but it hurt every time he brought it up.

"If it was up to me, you would be going out like some sort of knight of old, covered in armour."

Julia laughed. “More protective, but not very good for running through the streets. Come, it is time for bed now. We can rest easy, knowing that the couple the gang were targeting will be at home now, safe in their beds and none the wiser how close they came to disaster.”

“Just be mindful that thieves will not be happy about having their prey protected. They will not be honourable like the gentleman who caught you,” William cautioned.

“He was no gentleman. I managed to escape under my own steam,” Julia lied. It would not do her case or her cause any good if her uncle was to know just how vulnerable she had felt to be captured and held against a firm, muscled body. She could almost feel his arms still holding her tight, the most intimate she had been with any man. She had panicked in her efforts to get away, and that was not good for her long-term survival.

She vowed to do something the very next morning to increase her chances against such foes. It seemed she needed more than just Uncle William’s inventions if she was to be undefeated.

Chapter 2

"Ladies aren't allowed in here, miss." The bulk of a man stopped her entrance into the building so many others frequented.

Putting her hands on her hips, Julia squared up to him as much as she could against someone who seemed to fill a doorway. She was not small, nor thin, as was the fashion, her curves not being completely hidden even in an empire dress, but he towered over her in height and width. Holding her position, she refused to be daunted by him, which was clearly his intention.

"Show me where it says that women are not allowed," she said.

"It is just known," came the belligerent answer.

"You could be wrong, and Gentleman Jackson could be being prevented from earning even more money because you are a buffoon."

"That is not the way to persuade my staff to let you in," came the smooth, laughing voice of the owner of the Bond Street establishment.

“I beg pardon. I would not normally be so rude, but I have been stood here for fifteen minutes trying to persuade him to let me in,” Julia explained. She was a little overawed at coming face to face with the man himself, but she bit the inside of her cheek to try to focus her mind; she needed his help and was determined to get it. That, in some respects, he looked better dressed than some of the dandies tried to achieve only added to the aura that surrounded him. He was dressed in the finest clothing yet in an understated way; it was the attire of a man clearly sure of himself.

“Thank you, Bruce, you can let the young lady in. I will take it from here,” Jackson said.

“As you wish, sir.” It was clear he thought it a poor show that his master had not sent her away with a flea in her ear, and it wasn’t helped when Julia passed him, shooting a triumphant glance in his direction, which Jackson noticed.

“I have not agreed to your request, whatever it might be. I would not become too smug just yet,” Jackson said to Julia. “I let you in purely because I dislike a scene being caused on my doorstep; it is bad for business.”

Julia was fully aware that everyone who was anyone sought out the talents of this man. “I doubt that very much. Your reputation is far too illustrious for that to happen,” she responded, but her tone was not as confident or as combative as it had been with the doorman.

"Fiery piece, aren't you?" Jackson asked rhetorically, leading the way into a small office. He took a seat and indicated that Julia should sit in the chair opposite him. "Now, who are you, and what brings you here today?"

"My name is Miss Julia Marsh, and I need to learn how to protect myself and could think of no one better than you," Julia replied honestly.

"You have a difficult family member?" Jackson asked, eyebrows raised.

Julia was not surprised this man was renowned for his boxing ability. He oozed self-assuredness, having an air of confidence in his abilities that she envied, but his expression also seemed to hint that if she had said yes, he would have taken action to aid her. "No. It is for… Can we just say, in my line of work, I sometimes need to get out of tricky situations?"

Jackson crossed one leg over the other and looked at Julia shrewdly. "Do not insult my intelligence by trying to convince me that you are a lightskirt or some sort of doxy."

"No! It is nothing like that!" Julia flushed deep red, mortified that he would misinterpret her meaning. "I help out in the poorer areas, and it can be – challenging sometimes." Her words were met with silence as she was assessed with interest by Jackson, it made her want to squirm with discomfort, but she forced herself to remain poised, hands folded on her lap.

"Why are you helping when you are at risk?"

"It is the right thing to do. If I can help even a few people, then it is worth trying. I know I cannot do as much as I would wish." She was being scrutinised openly with his assessing stare, but she remained still. Too much depended on gaining his approval; the other night had brought that home to her. For the last two nights, she had dreamed of being wrapped in her captor's arms, and when she woke, she was disgusted to know that the dreams had leant towards being far too romantic for her liking.

"I suppose if you are doing good, it is my obligation to help you," he eventually said.

"Oh, would you? Thank you! I can pay," Julia said quickly.

"If you are helping the poor, I cannot make a profit from you, but does your family know what you are doing? I would not want a daughter of mine needing to learn how to box herself out of a situation."

"It is not just the poor I help, it is anyone who might be at risk. I do realise that my actions are causing my family to worry." He did not need to know that there was only her uncle at home. "This is why I am also going to visit next door to persuade them to teach me how to fence," Julia said.

Jackson burst out laughing. “I will do the introductions. I cannot wait to see the expression on my good friend Henry’s face when he realises we shall be teaching a fine young lady the base arts of defence. When would you like to start?”

“Now?” Julia asked hopefully.

“As you wish,” he responded, standing and pushing the chair and desk to one side.

For the next hour, Julia was put through basic paces by probably the best boxer in the world, certainly in the country. She followed his every direction, never questioning his reasoning as he corrected her moves, and was gratified that at the end of the hour of instruction, he took off his jacket and sparred with her for a few moments.

“You are a fast learner and a willing student,” Jackson said, shrugging back into his frock coat. He looked as cool as he had at the start of the hour, whereas Julia was feeling the effects of the exertion, her curls hanging limply at the side of her face, her cheeks aflame with the exercise and body far hotter than was comfortable.

“Thank you, although I do not think I will be able to move my arms tomorrow,” Julia admitted, putting her bonnet back in place and pulling on her gloves. Her arms felt shaky as she picked up her reticule.

"As I doubt you spend your days doing needlework, I think you will manage," Jackson responded.

Julia smiled. "No, I am probably better at fencing than I am at sewing, and I have never picked up a sword in my life."

Laughing, Jackson shook his head at her. "I will speak to Henry and arrange for your first lesson. Leave details of your abode here, and I will send a note round of the times you should be here or with Henry."

"Can I be assured of your confidentiality with regards to my training?" Julia asked, reluctant to give him her direction for fear her activities might be revealed. He might be indulging her, but the ladies of the *ton* would certainly see it in a different light, especially as she had come to a gentleman's club without chaperone or maid.

"A gentleman never tells, and I would most certainly be out of business if I started discussing with the wider population those who train with me," Jackson said.

Julia nodded, accepting his word and quickly wrote the address of the house in Half Moon Street. "Thank you for today; you cannot know how much it will help."

"You are quite intriguing, Miss Marsh. I hope one day to find out what is really going on with you."

Julia did not answer as she would do anything she could to keep her activities secret. It was her quest and hers alone; there would be no benefit in anyone knowing the truth, and it could put her more at risk if they did. No, she was determined that for once Gentleman Jackson would know very little about his student.

***

"You are missing another ball? Are you mad? This is the start of the season, when the best debutantes are still available. You know how soon the good ones get snatched up," John Carmichael said to his best friend as they walked through Green Park.

"If I was intent on marrying, your words would certainly sway me, but I have other more pressing matters to attend to," Hugh responded.

"The tip-off you received?" John asked. He was the only one in their circle who knew who Hugh was searching for.

"Yes. I have the Runners working on it, but I feel better if I am also doing my bit. The balls and debutantes can wait."

"Just remember that lightskirt of yours will eventually get tiresome; they always do. Best to get yourself a wife so you won't have the trouble of finding another mistress," John said.

"She has already become a bore," Hugh admitted of the woman he had thought had a similar outlook on life as he and annoyed that she had not. He was beginning to realise that no woman said what they actually meant, and it was frustrating, wasting all of their time.

"Started talking about marriage, has she?" John chuckled.

"I thought being a widow, she would be different, turns out she's nothing but a conniving shrew, albeit a pretty one."

"They are all the same when chasing a title and a fortune. You have it all, my friend, and you are passably good-looking too," John teased. "If you married, you would no longer be chased by every matchmaking mama who was in town; surely that is a temptation to become leg-shackled?"

"Fine praise indeed, my friend. But as much as being left alone sounds appealing, it still does not make me wish for marriage," Hugh said.

"You need an heir."

"No. I. Do. Not. I already have one, who I will trace if it takes me the remainder of my days."

"Sorry," John apologised at the thunderous response his comment had caused, knowing how much time and effort his friend was putting into finding his missing relative. "I hope you find her too, but you have to face facts. Even when you do find her, you will marry one day, and she will not inherit."

"She will inherit her portion whether I am foolish enough to have children of my own or not."

John decided it was time to change the subject if he wanted to keep his friend in his current reasonable mood. "Have you seen my new toy?" he asked, waving his cane at Hugh.

"You clearly had no soldiers to play with as a boy if that is your idea of a good toy," Hugh responded, side-stepping to avoid the cane, which was being swung around in a precarious fashion.

"Watch this," John said, raising the cane before touching the top, causing something to shoot out from the bottom and hit the nearest tree.

"What the devil is that?" Hugh asked.

"A small blade shot by the force of some contraption or other. Not quite sure how it works, but it's brilliant, is it not?"

"I have seen canes with a blade in the top or bottom, but why would you have a blade to shoot out when there are guns?"

"Have you not heard about the robberies that keep occurring?" John asked. "I refuse to carry a gun to every party or rout that I attend, but this is perfect to aid me if I should be accosted on my way home."

"It must have cost a lot. Would a blade not be cheaper?"

“No, that is the expected method of attack, but with this, I can release the blade first and ask questions later. It saves anyone getting too close,” John said.

Hugh was silent for a moment while John retrieved his blade. John presumed it was because his friend was impressed with his weapon, but Hugh was remembering the woman he had dealt with two nights ago. He wondered if she had been out on the streets again. He had considered going out himself the next night to see if he could find her but then had ridiculed himself for his nonsensical thoughts. She was probably someone out of bedlam, at very least a fool; no one with any sense would put themselves so much at risk.

When John retrieved the blade and fixed it back into position, Hugh nodded to the cane. “Who made that for you?”

“I knew you would appreciate it, could help get you out of any tricky situations you might come across in these places you insist on searching,” John said. “An inventor makes them. He is a bit eccentric, but his work is brilliant. Parker introduced me to him at the Fitzgerald’s ball last week.”

Hugh rolled his eyes. Parker was a ninnyhammer of the worst kind, always full of nonsense and hoping to discover the next trend of fashion. That he was ridiculed by most of the *ton* never seemed to dampen his enthusiasm. “I take it Parker has one for every day?”

John laughed. "How did you guess? But for once, with these robberies taking a more sinister turn, I think he could be onto a good thing."

"You will have to introduce me to this inventor of yours," Hugh said.

"Good. We can wait until we see him at a ball, or we can call around to number eight Half Moon Street. I will rest easier knowing you have all the weapons you can at your disposal," John said.

"You worry too much."

"One of us has to," John said, unusually serious.

Chapter 3

William entered the drawing room with a smile on his face. "I have just got another commission for the new canes."

"You are supplying the whole of the *ton* with deadly weapons," Julia responded, not completely at ease with the thought.

"If there was not the demand, I would not be selling any. And they probably end up sitting in a hallway somewhere and never used. You know what people are like, wanting the newest thing purely for the novelty of it," William said. "This request is interesting, though; the gentleman wants two, one for him and one for a lady."

"I do not envy that lady. What a poor present indeed! I would prefer a present of flowers, just in case you get any ideas about supplying me with a cane for my next birthday," Julia warned.

"Tsk, you know I would not dare give you anything that could harm another human being, you would never use it," William said. "It is great news, though. If the ladies start to order them, I will have enough funds coming in to concentrate on the inventions you do approve of."

"I have told you time and again that I am happy to fund your research. I believe in what you do," Julia said.

"And I have told you that I am not the type of guardian who will spirit away his ward's inheritance."

"You have not been my guardian for these last five years," Julia pointed out. "And you have given me a home and security when I needed it the most, which is priceless."

"In that case, you can repay my kindness by not casting me off in my old age; that is all the thanks and payment I need." William smiled at his niece. "Now, I have been thinking about ways of protecting you if you get grabbed from behind."

"My lessons with Gentleman Jackson and Mr Angelo are to prepare me for that eventuality if it happens again," Julia said.

"It is always good to have an alternative at your disposal. What if I fit your boots with spikes? You could do some damage to ankles and knees."

"Uncle, I will not be able to run quietly with spikes clattering behind me," Julia laughed. "The ability to run away has got me out of some tricky situations; I would not like to lose how quietly I can move."

"What about spikes at your elbows?" William offered. "That could work even better."

Julia pondered the option. She was not completely blasé about being out in a dangerous part of London, alone and at night. She did not want to carry weapons that could kill, but anything that stopped her from being caught and attacked would help to keep her safe. “Do not make them too big. If I have them attached to my clothing, I want it to be a surprise enough that they instinctively let go of me. I don’t want to impale someone on my arm.”

The smile she received convinced Julia that she had made the right decision, and she was happy to have hopefully eased some of the worries she knew her uncle suffered from when she was out.

“Excellent. I shall have something ready by tomorrow for you to look at,” William said.

“Good. I will be going out the day after. I can have a practice with them in the morning before we attend the ball at the Williams’ house,” Julia said.

“I worry tiredness will cause you to make a mistake.”

“Attending the odd ball is not going to affect the way I can run; in fact, the dancing will keep me in good practice.” Julia thought back to the other night and how her lungs felt like they would explode. She had wished there was somewhere she could go to practice running, but it would shock the gentlefolk of London if she were to lift her skirts and run. Blasted ladylike behaviour constantly got in the way.

***

"You've taken to teaching schoolgirls now, have you?" Hugh mocked Jackson as they circled each other in the ring. A large crowd had gathered around; any time Jackson fought it stopped all action in the building as everyone was keen to watch the master at work.

"She's no schoolgirl and could teach you a thing or two," Jackson responded, ignoring the barb Hugh had uttered to try to gain a small advantage over his opponent.

"I am averse to hitting women."

"You would be lucky to land a single punch; she's fast on her feet, nimble too," Jackson acknowledged.

Hugh frowned at the words, and his momentary lack of concentration cost him dearly. He picked himself up off the cushioned floor after the punch he had received because of his distraction. The crowd had been delighted to see him floored, and it had caused much heckling from the audience.

"What is she like?" he asked, standing and preparing to fight once more.

"Why?"

"I met someone a few nights ago, and it might be the same chit."

"She isn't one of your lightskirts, my lord," Jackson said, taking another swing, but one which Hugh blocked.

"I do know other women than lightskirts."

"That's not what I heard." Jackson grinned and landed another punch, but Hugh struck hard in retaliation. "Touché, my lord. Well aimed."

"Who is she?"

"That, sir, is nothing for you to worry about, whereas my left hook is quite another matter." Jackson brought their chatter to an end, increasing the ferocity of the attack on Hugh. The younger man had to use all his skill to ward off the blows that rained down on him.

Two hours later, Hugh still felt that he had suffered the beating of his life as he left the club with John. His attention was drawn by a young woman leaving the club next door, the hood of her cloak up as she climbed into a hackney waiting for her.

"John, I need to leave you. Something has come up," Hugh said, whistling to his carriage across the road.

"What has? You said you would accompany me to White's. What's got into you? Afraid of the ribbing you will get? You held your own with Jackson; you've nothing to fear," John said, not having noticed the woman.

"It isn't that," Hugh said. "I will see you later, John. Follow that hackney!" he shouted to his driver before jumping up onto the seat next to his servant. If he had not been concentrating so hard on not losing sight of the much smaller vehicle, he would have been amused at the shock on both his coachman's and his best friend's face, as the most particular Earl of Bryn jumped onto the seat as if he was a mere footman.

Hugh might have acted in haste, but he certainly repented at leisure about his choice of seat. The cool air seeped through his frock coat and waistcoat as it approached an hour of him sitting alongside his coachman. More than once, he considered calling the chase off, but he had a hunch that he was pursuing the woman who wandered the streets of London at night. It was too much of a coincidence for it to be otherwise.

As they headed to Mayfair, he started to doubt himself. Yes, she had not sounded like a local of the area he had met her in, but she surely could not be a gentlewoman? Not with the language she had used against him when she had cursed him. He did not know where he expected her to go, but it certainly was not to one of the nicest areas in London.

When they eventually turned into Half Moon Street, Hugh had come to the conclusion that he would never be warm again but was finally rewarded when the young woman climbed out of the hackney. Although his carriage did not stop, his coachman slowed right down, continuing at a leisurely pace past the house she had entered.

"Well, well, well," Hugh said to himself. "Isn't that interesting?"

The driver stopped the carriage as soon as they turned the corner, and Hugh jumped down. "Let's get home and as quickly as you can," he instructed as he climbed into the body of the carriage. Pulling out the blankets stored under the seat, he encased himself in them, teeth chattering all the way home.

Chapter 4

Julia fidgeted a little as she walked silently through the streets. She always got a hackney to take her as far as she could into the area she wanted to be. She would be wrapped in a cloak, which she would then hide in some place or other. It did not always prove a foolproof plan as she had lost more than one cloak but consoled herself with the thought that the person who had taken it probably needed it more than she did. It was a small price to pay to keep her activities quiet.

She focused on the areas that held the most balls and entertainments or the streets behind those places. It was usually after a long night of revelry that the aristocracy would wander from familiar streets and find themselves in less salubrious areas and with people who took advantage of every opportunity they spied. That robberies occurred on the main streets, too, she could not help with; it would risk her being revealed, and her reputation would be in tatters if that happened.

Julia never felt she was missing out on attending the balls; she did go to some, just not as many as a spinster of six and twenty years probably should do if she ever wanted to marry. Unfortunately, while this need to help people in trouble burned within her, all ideas of marriage and children were pushed away.

Blending into the background of the buildings as she walked down the streets, she was more alert than she had been the other night. That slip could have cost her, and she was not about to make the same mistake again.

A cry of distress rang out, and Julia started to run, keeping as close to the buildings as she could. It was only a matter of moments before she turned the corner onto the street the cry had originated from. Two robbers were confronting a couple, the woman holding her neck with one hand and clinging onto her husband with the other.

"You have the necklace, now let us go," the gentleman said. Julia could tell he was trying to sound more confident than he felt, as there was a slight tremble to his voice.

"This is good stuff, now give us any other trinkets you have."

"I only have my wedding ring; please do not take that," the woman cried.

"You can always get another," the lead robber said.

"It was my mother's," the woman sobbed. "It cannot be replaced."

"That's a shame, but we all have to eat," the robber said.

"And that necklace will feed you for a month, so I suggest you leave now, or I will be forced to make you give the necklace back," Julia said from the shadows. She had perfected the trick of lowering her voice, but many were not fooled into thinking that she would be any threat to them, sensing the voice was not from a large man.

"I would like to see you try," the robber mocked. "Are you the one they are calling the shadow? Come and show yourself."

"After you have let these good people go," Julia said.

"We haven't finished with them yet," the robber said. "I want that ring."

"That's a shame. Just remember that I did give you the chance to leave," Julia sighed, moving slightly out of the shadow of the building, prepared for battle. It would be the first time she tried all her new tricks, and she just hoped she had practised enough.

The robber laughed when he saw the figure dressed in black, including a mask covering most of her face. "You are a fool who is going to lose his life tonight. Are you ready to meet your maker?"

"I am ready to bring this to a close. Either leave with the necklace or leave with nothing." Julia saw the man and woman slowly start to move away, trying to put distance between them and the robbers without drawing attention to themselves, which was what she wanted to happen. The sooner they got away, the quicker she could make her own escape.

The two robbers laughed at Julia's words and moved towards her in an attempt to surround her, but she was ready for them, not waiting until they were in position to start the attack. Instead of dealing with the one approaching her from the front, she spun and landed a left hook on the second, who was circling her, trying to get to the rear. His head was flung backwards as the force of the punch hit its target, and blood spurted from his nose.

Having only one opponent for a moment at least, Julia took out a folded cane and flicked it out to full-length; she then parried with it as if it was a sword, landing blow after blow on the robber facing her. Blunt her instrument might be, but she had already benefited from six lessons from the master of fencing, and the hits landed with good effect.

The second robber came from behind, his roar of anger giving way to a yelp of pain as Julia's spikes connected with his stomach. She glanced around and was relieved to see that the couple had escaped whilst her fight had been going on. It was time for her to leave. With a swift jump out of the way of the two temporarily incapacitated men, she set off at a run.

There was no benefit in prolonging the attack; once the couple was safe, she had achieved her aim.

Eventually stopping to catch her breath, assuming all was safe, she folded up the cane and popped it back into its pocket. It had proved ideal tonight, and she allowed herself a moment of satisfaction before assessing how to get home. Her stamina was not enough to fight one battle after another, especially with different men who would be fresh for a fight. She would like to do more but knew her limitations.

Hearing a noise nearby, she shrank into the brickwork, at one with the building as much as anyone could be. A gentleman walked within a few feet of her, and she knew instinctively that this was the man who had disturbed her the last time she was out. It was clear he had not noticed her, and intrigued as to why he was in the area for a second time, she decided to follow him.

Not one usually to interfere in another's business, she was curious to find out who he was. Her footsteps made no sound as she padded behind him, far enough if he should turn around, she could make her escape without finding herself in a similar situation she had the last time their paths had crossed.

She could detect dejection in his demeanour and wondered if he had been robbed, but she dismissed the thought. Even in the darkened streets, she could tell he was dressed pristinely, something which no one could claim after being roughed up, and suspecting he would not give up without a fight, her curiosity increased as to what brought him here.

He was not trying to hide the fact he was a gentleman, a risky business in the areas he was frequenting, but continued to walk, casually swinging his cane. The moonlight reflected off his buttons when he turned a corner, and she could see his profile.

He was eventually approached by a man who appeared from the shadows, and after a quick conversation, something was exchanged, and the stranger continued on his way.

Turning another corner, Julia was surprised to see a carriage of the finest calibre, its crest covered, but the number of footmen on the carriage showed this was not the vehicle of a man of limited means. Julia waited in the shadows until he climbed into the carriage and left the area.

It was past time that she should be at home as her uncle would be worried. She wanted to follow the carriage, but it would take time to find a hackney, and she could not keep up with four horses on foot. So, feeling unsatisfied about her lack of knowledge about the stranger, she continued in the shadows, making her way to safety. His intriguing actions would have to be pondered over another day.

***

As he opened the morning paper, a small article caught Hugh's eye. *The Shadow Saves Again* was the title, and reading it, he guessed the young woman had been out the same night as he had. The article gave no hint that the hero who was the saviour in the story was a woman; in fact it described a man. He wondered if the description of two attackers was correct, and if it was, there was a spark of admiration, for the woman he had followed was not one who appeared able to fight off two assailants.

One thing was for sure, if she frequented the streets as much as the article suggested, she might have information that could help him. Ignoring the fact that she had stirred his interest for other reasons than needing her local knowledge, he determined to call on her household to force an introduction. He had been introduced to the cane maker, so a call would be perfectly acceptable. Ringing the bell for his carriage, he determined that there was no time like the present to officially make her acquaintance. It would be interesting to see her face, for he was fully aware of what her body felt like, even though he had never yet seen her features.

William Marsh was welcoming when Hugh was announced. He had completed the two canes which had been ordered from him and greeted the earl with the presumption that was the reason for the call.

After examining the canes and approving of them, Hugh got to the point. "There is a young lady who resides here. Is she your daughter?" he asked.

"No. My niece," William answered.

"I would like to make her acquaintance," Hugh said.

"And why would that be, my lord?" William asked. He was fully aware of Hugh's position, influence and reputation as a rake, so he was naturally very protective of Julia.

"To make her a present of this cane, of course," Hugh said, indicating one of the adapted canes he had ordered. William was clearly taken aback by the words, causing Hugh to smile in a derogatory fashion. "If she wanted to keep her identity a secret, she should take more care when taking her training sessions."

"I have no idea what you are referring to, my lord, and would be obliged if you would leave my home. You can have the canes with my compliments," William said stiffly.

"I am afraid I cannot comply with your request," Hugh responded. His tone was pleasant, but there was steel in his eyes. "I need to speak to your niece; she might have some information that would be of use to me. And, further, even if you will not protect her, it is my responsibility as a gentleman to give her this cane to help on what can only be considered a fool's errand when she is out alone and unprotected."

William stood straighter, his face infused with a flush of anger. "How dare you come into my home and speak to me in such a fashion! As if I have not tried to dissuade her from her quest. And you insult me if you think I would create weapons for the likes of you and allow my niece to go out without the best I can provide."

"She could not defend herself a few weeks ago when I surprised her." His words were said with derision. The uncle could fool himself as much as he liked, but Hugh knew just how vulnerable a respectable young woman was on the streets of London.

"It was you who accosted her, was it? I wondered who it was, especially as she said she was convinced he was a gentleman, but she has taken extra precautions since then," William said, but the fight had gone out of him. Worried that Julia's reputation was about to be ruined, he could not argue against the same feelings being expressed by Hugh.

"And what happens the next time she is surprised? With the newspapers reporting on her, every nodcock in London and every criminal will see it as good sport to take her down. They do not know she is but a chit of a girl," Hugh said.

"I would say at six and twenty, I am far beyond being considered a chit," Julia's voice came from the doorway.

Both men turned, and Hugh could finally see the woman he had not been able to forget since their first meeting. She had black hair and deep brown eyes framed with long lashes. Her figure was tall, coming to his shoulder, which he had not realised when lifting her off the ground; it explained why his boots had been so dirty, though, her being tall enough to trample all over his feet. Her features were handsome rather than pretty, but her expression was not one of welcome as she glared at him.

"Julia, this is the Earl of Bryn. My lord, this is my niece, Miss Julia Marsh," William introduced, silently admitting defeat.

Hugh bowed. "Miss Marsh."

"I would say it was a pleasure to meet you, my lord, but I have heard enough to know we have absolutely nothing more to say to each other. Therefore, I bid you good day and would ask that you leave my home," Julia said.

"There is something I wish to discuss with you," Hugh said.

"Nothing that would be of interest to me. You may be able to intimidate my uncle, my lord, but my butler is far less particular about who he throws out, and I have all the weapons at my disposal, including this cane you so obligingly had made for me," she said, having quickly crossed the room and grabbed the end of the cane before stepping out of reach.

"Julia! He is a peer of the realm," William appealed.

"Who is trying to threaten and intimidate me in my home. I will not allow it, now or ever," Julia responded, never taking her eyes off Hugh.

Knowing when he was at a disadvantage, he would not be able to ask her questions whilst she was in such an unobliging frame of mind, he decided to leave. Annoyed that it would be seen as a retreat due to the weapon she was aiming in his direction, he bowed stiffly.

"This is not over, Miss Marsh. We shall speak soon."

"Not if I have anything to do with it," Julia said to his disappearing form.

"Oh, Julia," William moaned when the front door closed. "When will you consider your reputation?"

Chapter 5

Entering the ballroom, Julia half expected to receive the cut direct if the Earl of Bryn had been spreading what he knew of her, but she was surprised and more than a little relieved to find her welcome as it usually was.

Approaching her good friend Serena, she embraced her, and they stood at the side of the ballroom catching up with each other. Their parents had been friends, but beyond that Serena was part of the group to which Julia belonged.

"Have you seen the news?" Serena asked. "Every day the shadow is out protecting the streets; it helps me to rest easier knowing that he is out there. I realise robberies happen everywhere, but they do seem to be coming closer to the streets I have always felt safe on."

"You should not believe everything you read," Julia said. She was uncomfortable lying to her friend, but even if Serena believed it if Julia confessed to her, she could not take the risk of losing any of her friends; they were too precious to her.

"But it names the people who have been saved," Serena argued. "How can they make it up if there are members of the *ton* telling their stories?"

"I do not know," Julia replied honestly. She had only been out once more that week, when she had seen but not been seen by the Earl of Bryn. The papers were reporting something about the shadow's exploits every day.

They were interrupted by the unexpected arrival of Hugh at their side. "Miss Marsh, would you do me the honour of dancing the next with me?" he asked with a bow.

"I do not intend to dance tonight, but I thank you, my lord," Julia responded, dropping a curtsey.

"But, Julia, you have told me that you have the quadrille with Ben!" Serena said of her cousin, with whom she was hopeful her friend would make a match. She also saw the advantage in her friend dancing with an earl. At their ages, they had to consider all options.

Julia saw the gleam of triumph in Hugh's eyes and wished she could use her elbow spikes to pierce his feeling of superiority. "Silly me," she responded in a fake tinkling voice. "Of course, I would be delighted to dance with you, my lord. I can think of nothing I should like more."

Hugh smiled, but it was genuine, not the smile of triumph Julia had expected. It did not help settle her inner feelings towards him; she could clearly see why he was so sought after when his blue eyes lit with amusement, and the smile made him seem younger and less cynical. For some reason, the thought that she had been the one to break through his cold exterior and amuse him caused something to stir inside her, but she quickly got control of herself. She was aware of his reputation, even though she had not officially met him previously, and she was not about to turn into a simpering miss just because of one endearingly attractive smile.

"Miss Marsh," Hugh said, offering his arm.

"Lord Bryn," Julia responded.

They took their places in the dance, and Hugh smiled once more. "I am looking forward to having the most delightful of partners; anyone who is so light on their feet can only be a good dancer. Ah, do not glare at me, Miss Marsh. It was a genuine compliment," he chuckled.

"If it is your aim to try and upset my equilibrium, I am afraid you have chosen the wrong partner," Julia responded.

"You do me a disservice, Miss Marsh. I am merely looking forward to the next half an hour. You must admit that our first meeting was not conducive to getting to know each other, nor was our second come to that."

"No, but it did make me realise that you like to interfere when not wanted."

"Oh, come now. I still argue the point that you had no real plan," Hugh said.

Julia's eyes narrowed, not liking the way he was right in that instance. "I do not approach many situations where I have not assessed every eventuality. I would be foolhardy to do otherwise."

"That I am glad to hear," Hugh said, for the moment being serious. "I must admire your stamina; to have been out every night this week is a feat indeed."

"I have not been. The last time I was out, I followed you to your carriage, unseen of course." She was pleased with the look of surprise her words caused, glad that he too could be disconcerted.

"That was four nights ago," he said.

"I am aware of that. It seems the newspapers are making the stories up, or someone else is copying what I am trying to do," Julia admitted. She was reluctant to acknowledge it to herself, but it was good to be able to speak to someone about her work, other than her uncle. He was driven by worry, and although she could detect a hint of concern from Hugh, which came as a surprise to her, it was a relief to discuss the news reports which had been causing her disquiet.

"It could make you more vulnerable. You will become a target if you are not already," Hugh said.

"I know, but I cannot stop."

"What is it you hope to achieve?"

"What are you wishing to achieve?" Julia asked, trying to deflect the questions away from herself. "You have to admit, wandering around in the middle of the night in the areas you frequent is not a normal pastime for someone of your calibre."

"Some would argue that I am not a normal member of the *ton*," Hugh said, equally reluctant as Julia to confess all.

Julia smiled. "You said that, not I."

"I thought it wise to not give you the chance to insult me further."

"Spoilsport," Julia responded.

"I must say, I prefer your attire this evening to wearing, let us say, an *interesting* choice of outfit the other night," Hugh changed the subject.

Julia flushed. "It helps to be as inconspicuous as possible," she hissed at him, not wishing the other dancers to hear what they were speaking of. As they were in a long-ways set, most people concentrated on their own partners; it would have been different if the dance was a cotillion or quadrille.

"I am sorry to be the bearer of bad news, but it was as plain as a pikestaff that you were a female as I watched you move."

Having the strangest feeling inside at the thought of him watching her, she managed to look loftily at him. "Not everyone is as observant as you. So far, I have been considered nothing more than a man."

"That is something only a fool would believe when looking at you."

Julia was glad that the dance ended at that point. His words seemed to suggest a compliment, but she had no quick retort to throw back at him. Even if she had some response, for once she wanted to accept the praise. It was a strange feeling, for she would never consider herself vain, but to hear the words of admiration from probably the most handsome man in the room was something to savour. When they honoured each other at the end of the dance, she felt a pang of regret that their time together had flown by.

Hugh offered his arm, but before they moved away from their fellow dancers, they were approached by a woman who was smiling at Hugh. Julia felt the muscles stiffen under her hand, which rested on Hugh's arm, and she glanced curiously at the newcomer.

"Hugh, my love, I did not know you were attending tonight. You should have let me know," the woman purred.

Julia was amused that she had been looked over and clearly dismissed as someone of little importance before the woman had turned her full attention onto Hugh.

"I did not realise I needed to inform you of my every commitment," Hugh responded coldly.

The woman blinked at the rebuttal she had received in front of another but maintained her smile.

It was a little strained, but she was clearly trying to disguise the fact that she was not used to being spoken to in such a way. “I thought that is what friends did.”

“You stopped being my friend when you tried to engineer a compromising situation between us,” Hugh responded.

His words caused the woman to glance in mortification at Julia, who felt a modicum of pity that her business was being aired in front of her. She decided to be gracious and let the woman and Hugh sort their differences out without her acting the observer. “It seems you have things to discuss, and I am an unwanted third. Please excuse me; I see my friends have arrived,” Julia said.

“I shall escort you,” Hugh said.

“There really is no need,” Julia insisted before walking away without looking back at the pair. The woman had looked older than Hugh; Julia was wise enough to guess she had been or was his mistress. Pushing aside any opinion she might have on the matter, for it was really none of her business, she smiled at her group of friends. “Good evening, ladies. How are my favourite Bluestockings doing?”

There were six ladies in the gathering, including Julia, most around the same age as she was, but there was one who was older, in her forties. She was the founder of the group and well respected by the others.

"You did not attend the club last week," Alice, the one nearest to Julia, said of their fortnightly Bluestocking Club meeting.

"No, Uncle was working on something new, and you know how he gets when he is in his invention frame of mind, he needs me by his side," Julia lied. She had actually been practising with Gentleman Jackson but could never confess to it, even though her friends were more like sisters to her.

"At the next meeting we have an interesting speaker, Caroline Herschel. She's going to talk to us about her astronomical discoveries," Grace, the eldest woman, said.

"That will be fascinating. I promise I will be there, honestly, Grace," Julia said to the older woman. "You know I do not miss our gatherings lightly."

"You have been distracted these last few months," Grace said.

"I have, but I promise it is nothing to worry about."

"You would come to us if it were, wouldn't you?" Alice asked.

"Of course," Julia said but did not meet Grace's appraising stare. Sometimes she suspected that Grace could read minds, and not for the first time she wondered if the older woman suspected something of what she was doing.

"You seem to have made a hit with your dancing partner," Grace said, thankfully changing the subject. "He seemed quite enamoured whilst you were dancing. I wish someone would look at me the way he was looking at you."

"I think you mean he spent the half-hour glaring at me," Julia laughed.

"Why would he glare at you?"

"He is no friend of mine, more like an annoyance than anything else," Julia responded, refusing to acknowledge that she had been affected by her dance with the handsome yet intriguing earl and then disappointed by the approach of the stranger, which she knew was ridiculous. He was nothing to her and never could be, but that thought also made her feel somewhat sad. Inwardly chiding herself for her foolishness, she smiled at her friend. "Alice, I have not seen you since you went to the new exhibition at the National Gallery. Was it worth a trip?"

***

Hugh took a step back as if he had been struck. An annoyance? He had been dismissed with two cutting words by a spinster? He could not believe what he had heard.

Having got rid of Kathryn, who had only approached to find out who he was dancing with and to cause trouble, he cursed to himself that he should have known better than to start any relationship with her. To his shame, he acknowledged that he had never had feelings for her and that he suspected she felt nothing for him did not assuage his guilt in allowing a relationship to develop. The only good thing, although it was unfortunate for Kathryn, was that he knew he had already been replaced in her affections by some other man with deep pockets for an expensive mistress. Kathryn no longer wanted him, she just enjoyed causing trouble wherever she went. It was another reason he should have kept his distance.

Hugh's aim once Kathryn had been dealt with had been to apologise to Julia for Kathryn's interruption, but on approaching, he heard Julia's opinion of him and was now reeling from her revelation.

A man more likely to give out criticism suddenly realised how being on the receiving end could sting. He walked away from the group, unseen but seething. How dare she insult him without just cause? He had done nothing but try to protect the chit since he had met her. Experiencing feelings that had never troubled him before, he stung with the rebuttal.

The feelings incensed him, and for a moment he allowed the anger to overtake his shock and surprise. He could ruin her by a whisper here and there, and she would be the laughing stock of society. She deserved it.

It surprised him how much he was affected by her words and what hurt they caused. Was it that he expected her to be flattered by his attentions? Probably, he acknowledged, for the first time realising how the attentions of others had inflated his own sense of worth. It was a sobering realisation but enough to make him ponder.

Walking to the edge of the ballroom, still feeling stunned from what he heard of another's opinion of himself, Hugh admitted that Julia deserved none of his vitriol towards her. She had asked for nothing from him and, in fact, had made it perfectly clear that she did not wish his interference, help or attention. It was he who had pursued her, not the other way around, which again was a strange occurrence for Hugh.

Why could he not get her out of his mind as easily as she could him? He stood blindly watching the dancers, pondering if he was just being a good citizen by trying to protect a foolish girl from being attacked or if there was more to his interest. He was beginning to suspect that he wasn't just being altruistic, which was more of a worry than any of his other musings.

Thankfully, John interrupted his thoughts before he could acknowledge something as foolish as a serious liking for Julia, which would never do as he was certainly not in the habit of chasing after irritating spinsters. He turned to his friend with relief.

"I see you have taken pity on one of the bluestockings," John said as he stood beside Hugh.

"The bluestockings?"

"You are out of society far too much," John chastised. "The group of women over there, with your last dancing partner. They are all members of the Bluestocking Club, which sounds just about the most unappealing club you could ever come across. They do all sorts of exciting things like discuss books and invite people to come and speak to them."

"And Miss Marsh is a member?" Hugh wondered if all the bluestockings were involved in similar activities but doubted it as he assessed the other six women. One was too old to be scampering around the London streets at night, two were not built for running, but the others might be in cahoots with Julia. They had not come to her aid when he had first met her, so either they went to different areas, or Julia acted alone. The thought made a lump of lead form in his stomach. He hated the idea that she might be overpowered one day. Cursing his feelings after Julia had so clearly dismissed him to the others, he turned his attention back to his friend.

"Yes. My sister says most of the other women are intimidated by them; they would rather talk about the latest developments in the sciences than the latest fashions," John said with a shudder.

"None of them looks out of place here, so their taste in the latest attire cannot be criticised; their time is clearly spent on more interesting matters." For some reason, Hugh could not find fault with the group of women who Julia was connected to. It surprised him, and from the expression on John's face, it had equally affected his friend.

John spluttered at Hugh's words. "You would want a wife who demanded intelligent conversation over the breakfast table? I can barely utter two words until after luncheon. You may chase them, but I am staying far away, like most of the men in the room."

Hugh had noticed that the group of women, none of whom were Friday-faced or ape-leaders, were not surrounded by men. It could be because they were older or that they had no fortune; he did not know how rich or poor they were, but neither reason for their lack of attention rested easy with him.

Julia was challenging and extremely irritating, but she also had a fire within her that he was drawn to; surely others would be too? He was nothing special in that regard, seeing the same attractions the others of his acquaintance did.

His fascination with Julia would have to be tempered; it was a new experience for him and something he would have to be careful of. Casting off a mistress who had replaced him with a richer man was one thing, getting involved with an unmarried gentlewoman was quite another.

He certainly felt at sixes and sevens as he watched Julia laugh and joke with her friends, seeming unaffected or unconcerned about him. He determined to do the same as her, turning on his heel and leaving the ball to visit one of his clubs where his equilibrium would be restored and he could enjoy the company of like-minded men. He could no longer face a night of tediousness by remaining at the ball, his decision being based on the fact that he had danced with the most interesting woman in the room.

She was as annoying as she considered him to be, frustratingly enticing in both the disguise she wore and the beautiful blue silk gown that had enhanced her looks tonight. That she was putting herself at risk every time she ventured out would have him tossing and turning long into the night.

Chapter 6

"The shadow supposedly struck again last night," William said to his niece as he read the paper over breakfast.

"I have not been out for days, and still there are reports," Julia said. "I cannot continue this way. I have purposely stopped what I set out to do because of the foolish stories, but with them continuing, I am staying away when I could be helping."

"Perhaps it is for the best?" William suggested. "This way, the thieves and vagabonds know there is a threat to them, but you are not in any danger. I would think this is a perfect solution."

"But we do not know if another person or persons is impersonating me or if it is just rumours and made-up stories. If it is the latter, then people are still at risk," Julia argued.

"What can I say to dissuade you?"

"I am afraid there is nothing. Until I feel I have done all that I can, or until something changes, I must continue," Julia answered. There was nothing but sorrow in her tone; she hated the fact she was causing her uncle worry, but it was a drive within her that she could not help.

"I worry you will never move on and settle down with your life whilst you are chasing ghosts, Julia. Your parents would not have wanted this for your future," William said gently. It was the same sentence he repeated on a regular basis, but it never seemed to have any impact.

"They did not want any of it to happen, but sometimes life surprises us, and we must deal with it as best we can. I promise to continue to be careful. My lessons with both Gentleman Jackson and Mr Angelo are imparting skills I could never have hoped to have and are giving me a real advantage."

"You do carry yourself differently since you have begun working with them," William said.

"I feel different," Julia acknowledged. It was true; the lessons had made her stronger, more confident in her abilities and smoother in her movements.

"Just do not let it give you a false sense of invincibility," William warned.

"I will not," Julia promised.

***

As she leaned against a wall, gasping for breath, she remembered the conversation of that morning with a grimace. The fight she had just survived had been brutal and worse than anything she had experienced so far. It seemed the stories of the shadow were leading to more challenges than she had faced in the past. It had become a matter of honour for those she came across to defeat the person the newspapers had built into some sort of masked crusader.

Touching her face with her hand, she winced. She had never had a facer like the one which had struck home; it had sent her reeling, but fortunately her reactions had been quick to recover, and she had managed to roll away from further attack before using her cane.

Yes, she had accepted the cane that Hugh had commissioned for her. It had pleased her far more than she cared to admit that he would be concerned enough to have her uncle make a weapon she could use for protection. At first, she had not wanted to carry it, rehearsing her arguments about not wishing to hurt people, even those doing criminal acts. But William had tweaked the cane, making it smaller and with a weaker firing mechanism so that it would not inflict serious damage. Just enough to help her escape, as had happened tonight.

Not wanting to admit that the whole episode had been too close a call for her liking, she waited, fully aware of her surroundings, whilst letting her body calm after its exertion. The punch had shaken her badly, never having been on the receiving end of an attack before, she realised that she could not withstand such brutality and pain. Her face was throbbing, and for a moment she wanted to give in and let the tears fall, but she forced herself to remain focused. She could not afford to become vulnerable whilst still out; she could give in to the shock of what she had experienced when she was safe.

As she pushed herself off the wall, ready to make her way home, a scream rang out across the air and Julia, immediately forgetting that she did not get involved with a rescue more than once in an evening, ran towards the sound.

Faltering when she was faced with the scene, she tried to take in what was happening before acting in haste. She was at a disadvantage from already being tired and injured and had to decide carefully where best to help.

Hugh was fighting with two men, whilst a young woman who had clearly been the one to scream struggled with a third. No one needed to be an expert to know that Hugh would lose, no matter how good he was at fighting.

Deciding that she did not have the energy to make this an extended fight, Julia took out her fencing cane and started on the man who was trying to drag the young woman away. The sooner this was over for them all, the better.

Her surprise attack gave her the advantage, and she was more ruthless than usual as she went in for parry after parry until the man collapsed on the floor. A cane aimed for the ribs can inflict enough damage to incapacitate someone.

"You have one chance to run, or I finish this here," Julia growled at him, hoping the false reputation she now had would give some credence to her words.

The man looked at her before glancing at his friends. He stumbled to his feet, all the time moving away from Julia, and ran with speed down the street.

Not knowing if he would return with reinforcements, Julia immediately turned her attention to the other two men still attacking Hugh. But before she could react, the young woman had flung herself onto the back of one of the men and was pummelling and scratching him for all she was worth.

The man reacted by turning away from Hugh, trying to get the madwoman off his back. Julia moved in, punching him swiftly in the stomach with a left and right, stepping back as he crumpled to his knees.

"Leave him!" she shouted to the young woman still attacking the man. When there was a pause because of Julia's command, she poked her cane into the man's ribs, hard. "You have until I count to five to disappear, and we will forget you were ever here."

He glared at Julia but struggled to his feet. Turning to the young woman, he snarled at her. "This isn't over. We ain't done here; you owe me," he spat at the girl.

"I owe you nothing," the girl responded, hands on hips.

"Four!" Julia shouted, bringing the conversation to a close. The man spat at her before taking off and limping down the street in the direction his counterpart had gone.

Turning to Hugh, Julia was relieved to see the third man sprawled out on the road, clearly unconscious, and Hugh, although breathing heavily, was brushing himself down.

"It seems we meet again, Miss Marsh," Hugh drawled.

"You're a female?" the young woman asked, but before Julia could answer, Hugh had crumpled to his knees.

"What is it?" Julia asked, immediately by Hugh's side.

"I think I might be more injured than I thought," Hugh answered before collapsing on the ground.

The young woman started pulling at Hugh's frock coat. "No. No. No. I can't lose him when he's only just found me," she wailed.

"Wait here," Julia said. "I know his carriage will be close by; I shall seek assistance."

"No, let me. I know these streets better than you."

"What is your name?" Julia asked.

"Florry – Florence," came the answer. "And this is my uncle," she said of Hugh.

Julia did not respond to the news with any outward emotion. For some reason, the fact that the young woman was a relative came as a surprising relief, which she knew was foolish, but she had thought he had taken another mistress, and it had disappointed her in a way she had not expected to feel. Concentrating on Hugh, she nodded to Florence. "Please be quick, I'll try to stop the bleeding, but we do not know if the others will come back with more men."

Florence nodded and disappeared around the corner while Julia took off Hugh's cravat, ignoring the feel of his soft hair as her fingers moved the material around his neck. Now was not the time to indulge in her silly fantasies. She pressed it on the wound, which was at his side, from what she could see in the dim light of the night. If the amount of blood was anything to go by, the knife had not gone too deep; at least she hoped that was the case.

Before too long, Julia heard the sound of horses' hooves and breathed a sigh of relief. Hugh had stirred once and looked at Julia with confusion before closing his eyes again. She was not sure whether he was conscious or not, but she continued to mutter assurances to him in case he could hear her.

Footmen seemed to fill the street as they jumped to assist their master, and he was soon ensconced within the safety of the carriage. Julia stepped back, but Florence grabbed her arm. "Please come with us."

"It is not appropriate for me to be seen like this," Julia said, waving her hand at her outfit to emphasise the point. "Just keep the cloth on the wound until the doctor arrives; his servants will help."

"This is not my world. I don't know how things work in it. Please come with us, I beg of you," Florence pleaded.

In the light of the carriage, Julia could see the fear on Florence's face and that she was younger than Julia had first presumed. Hesitating for only a moment, Julia stepped forward. "I will need to send a message to my uncle or he will worry about my absence."

"Anything," Florence said, climbing into the carriage. "Thank you."

The steps were lifted, and the door closed behind them before the carriage moved off at speed.

***

Neither woman said anything at first while they travelled through the quiet streets of London. Julia had continued to tend to Hugh as Florence scrambled into a corner of the carriage, curling her legs underneath her and staring at her uncle.

Eventually the young woman spoke. “I should explain what happened.”

“It has nothing to do with me. I am just glad I was able to help in some way,” Julia said.

“Without your help, I don’t think they would have given up; we were losing the fight,” Florence said.

“It is unimportant now. All that matters is making sure your uncle is well.” The thought of him not surviving brought a lump of panic to Julia’s throat, which she managed to swallow without betraying her feelings.

“He cannot die, not now he has finally found me,” Florence said, sounding as upset as Julia felt. “I was always told that my family did not care, but he said he has been looking for me for such a long time, he had almost given up hope of ever discovering me. I can hardly believe that he tried to find me in the first place and has been searching for months and months.”

Julia looked with renewed interest at Hugh. She had presumed he was in the areas she frequented because he was visiting some bawdy house or gambling den – there were plenty to choose from – but it seemed she had misjudged him. She was curious to know more, but now was not the time.

“You are safe now,” Julia said.

"But it is true what I said, I have no idea about his world and how I will be received at the house. I beg of you to not leave me."

"I will stay until everything is settled, but you must know I cannot remain in a gentleman's house with only you as company. I might not fit into society as I would wish, but I do not want to be completely cast out."

"No. It is a very lonely place," Florence said.

"Where are your mother and father?"

"My mother is dead, she was my uncle's older sister, and I have no idea where my father is, he abandoned us a long time ago."

"I am sorry." The questions about how Florence had been surviving were none of Julia's business and it was probably best she did not know, but she felt sympathy for the girl. She could only imagine what struggles she had faced.

They arrived at Hugh's townhouse, and again there was a flurry of activity. To be fair to the butler, he did not give any sign of surprise that his master was being delivered unconscious and injured, accompanied by two young women, one dressed in clothes which were nothing more than rags and one dressed completely in black and wearing breeches.

In fact, he impressed Julia by looking at Florence and bowing his head. "Miss Florence, it is good to have you home at last," he said before leading them all into the warm house.

Florence looked at Julia. "I have no idea how he knows me," she confessed in a whisper.

"There is a family resemblance to your uncle, so I presume you must resemble your mother, and I suppose if he knew you were being looked for, it is not hard to make the connection."

"This is all terrifying," Florence said as they entered the house.

Julia breathed a sigh of relief once the front door had closed. She had abandoned her mask when dealing with Hugh, so did not want to be seen by any late revellers returning home. Waiting until the butler and valet had settled Hugh and the doctor had been sent for, she approached the butler.

"I need to send a message to my uncle, he will be worried about my lateness in returning home," she said.

"Of course, madam. If you would follow me, I will lead you to the study where you can write a note. I will have it delivered immediately. If you would also allow me to bring some ice for your face, I think it would be wise."

She self-consciously raised her fingers to her cheek and winced when touching the tender skin. "I had forgotten about this," she said.

"Best to try and reduce the swelling, although there will be bruising," the butler said matter of fact.

Julia was thankful that now the immediate urgency had passed, she saw no condemnation in his expression. He was obviously a butler who was not easily shocked. She wondered what he had seen to make him so blasé about the evening's events and decided that it was probably best she did not know.

It felt strange entering the study of the man who had been her tormentor these last few weeks, although she understood him more now she was aware of his search for Florence. The butler handed her paper and she sat and quickly scribbled a note to her uncle. What he would think when he received it, she did not wish to dwell on, but she was confident he would send some more suitable clothing.

While waiting for Uncle William to send her clothes, she returned to the bedchamber. Florence was seated by the side of Hugh's bed, but she rose when Julia entered.

"He is not awake and I need him to be. He cannot die now!" she cried.

Julia immediately crossed the room and embraced the young girl. "Everything will be done to care for him, but I do not think his wound is life-threatening. The bleeding was not too severe," she soothed.

"I am just so sick of being afraid," Florence confessed. "It is selfish of me I know, but tonight for the first time when he explained who he was and why he had found me, I felt that I could relax. That I did not have to live thinking what could go wrong and who I needed to avoid."

"You poor thing, it sounds like you were living a hellish life," Julia said. "You are safe here. The reception by the butler will ensure that all the staff will treat you with the respect you deserve. You have nothing to worry about."

"But if he dies, I will be alone again," Florence said, dissolving into tears.

The doctor and butler entered the room, both glancing at Florence and Julia. "Miss Florence is overwrought," Julia said to the butler. "I think a warm bed, hot chocolate and a little laudanum will help calm her and allow her to rest. She will feel better able to face everything when she is more refreshed in the morning."

"Certainly, madam," the butler said. "I gave instructions to prepare two bedchambers, and hot chocolate is ready on the stove as we speak."

"Perfect. Thank you," Julia said. "If you will direct me to Miss Florence's chamber, when she is settled, I will return to speak to the doctor. If that is acceptable?" She did not wish to be too pushy, but she knew that Florence was in no position to take control of the situation even though she was the one who was effectively in charge.

"Of course." The butler bowed his head and stepped outside the chamber to indicate the room Julia should take Florence. "Will you need a maid to assist you?"

"No. I think the fewer people Florence has to deal with for now, the better. She needs quiet."

Florence had not said a word, just clinging to Julia and quietly crying as they entered the bedchamber. She silently allowed Julia to help her undress, just leaving her chemise on to act as nightdress. She was then led to bed and tucked in.

A knock at the door made Florence jump, but Julia rested a reassuring hand on her shoulder. "I expect this will be your hot chocolate," she said. Crossing the room, she took the tray from the maid at the door, not wishing her to come inside. What the maid thought about the situation of her master being injured, a niece returned, and Julia wearing men's clothing, she did not dwell on. Things had taken a turn that could not be altered now. She would have to accept whatever the fall-out was of her being seen in such distinctive clothing and sporting a clearly visible bruise if the butler's reaction was anything to go by.

Nodding her thanks when the maid pointed out the vial of laudanum and a bundle of ice wrapped in a cloth, she closed the door with her foot and turned back to the room. "This will help give you a restful night and hopefully your uncle will be able to speak to you in the morning," Julia said to Florence.

Florence was deathly white and seemed far too small for such a large bed. Julia busied herself adding the sleeping draught to the drink, and once stirred in, she handed the cup to Florence.

"Thank you. I don't know what I would have done without you," Florence said meekly.

"Oh, I think you do not give yourself enough credit. You have clearly coped in worse situations than this, so I think you would have been fine," Julia soothed. "If you forgive my curiosity, how old are you?"

Florence glanced at Julia. "I tell everyone that I am over twenty, but I am sixteen."

"Dear child, you must have been terrified!" Julia could not stop herself from exclaiming. She knew girls of that age and they seemed so very young, certainly not capable of fending for themselves.

"It was safer to pretend I was older; some people prey on young girls and without any family to provide support..." Florence shrugged, leaving the rest of the words unsaid, but Julia was fully aware of what could happen to young, untouched girls who were unprotected.

"You are safe now, which means you can be yourself." Julia smiled at her. "And that is a girl who is going to sleep until she is refreshed and then eat for days before persuading her very rich uncle to buy her lots of clothes."

Florence laughed and put down the cup on the bedside cabinet. "That sounds wonderful. I am almost afraid to go to sleep for fear all this will have been some sort of dream when I awake."

"I promise you it will not and I will be here to make sure all is well," Julia said gently, moving the covers so Florence could wriggle further into the bed. She had hardly blown out the candles on the bedside cabinet when Florence's breathing settled into the steady rhythm of someone asleep.

Watching the young girl for a moment whilst pressing the cold cloth to her own cheek, Julia felt an almost maternal pull to her. What she had seen and experienced made Florence far more worldly-wise than Julia was, but yet she seemed so innocent in other ways. She was barely more than a child, and Julia hoped she would be allowed to be a silly young girl to make up for what she had been through. Florence needed fun in her life, and Julia hoped Hugh would realise that.

"Sweet dreams, Florence," she said before leaving the room and returning to Hugh.

Chapter 7

The doctor was packing up as Julia entered the room. She crossed to the opposite side of the bed, hoping it would cover up some of her outfit, still a little embarrassed at being seen in men's clothing and injured. She could do nothing about her face, but she could hide the fact that she was wearing breeches by standing beside the bed.

"How is he?" she asked.

"He has been very lucky," the doctor said. "The knife has glanced his side, missing everything of importance and not going in too deep. Not many people are so fortunate when faced with men intent on robbery."

"No." Julia knew that all too well.

"I have given him a draught just as a caution, but I expect him to be conscious and alert tomorrow if no fever sets in."

"He was barely conscious on the way here," Julia said. "Is that not unusual if his wound is not too bad?" Florence was not the only one who needed to know that Hugh would be well.

"It would have been caused by the initial shock of the incident and the blood loss. I believe you were the one stemming the flow. You did a good job, wounds like this do tend to bleed a lot when they are first inflicted," the doctor explained. "He is young and strong, perfectly capable of recovering fully, although he should remain in bed until the wound has completely healed."

"How long will that take?" Julia knew that Florence needed Hugh to support her and help her settle in to her new life.

"I would imagine at least a week, but it will depend on him. If he moves too soon, he could reopen the wound, so you need to give clear instructions," the doctor said. "Would you like me to take a look at your face?"

"No thank you. It is bruised, but I do not think there will be any permanent damage," Julia assured him. "I should have been quicker on my feet."

"It comes to something when a man will hit a young woman. Sometimes society disgusts me," the doctor said.

Julia was not convinced she completely suppressed the smile at the doctor's supposition of what had happened; she wondered what his opinion was of young women who roamed around in men's clothing. She tried to cover her amusement by inclining her head and thanking the doctor before nodding to the butler. The doctor was shown out of the chamber, leaving her alone with Hugh's valet.

"He will not rest willingly," the valet said.

"That does not surprise me; from what I have seen so far he is a stubborn mule." It was probably inappropriate to utter such words to a servant, but Julia was worn out with the events of the night. She was beginning to realise that the whole episode would take some explaining to her uncle, and she just did not have the energy now the initial rush of adrenaline was ebbing.

The butler returned quicker than Julia had expected. "Madam, there is a gentleman asking to see you urgently. He says he is your uncle."

"Uncle William is here?" Julia asked. "Oh dear, this is not good."

She followed the butler, who this time led her to what must be a morning room. The fact that it was the middle of the night and every sensible person was safely tucked up in bed did not seem to matter in Hugh's household. The room was lit as it would be during the evening, and the fire was going.

Julia entered the room, and her heart sank as she watched her uncle pace across the room in obvious agitation. As soon as he saw her his shoulders sagged in relief, but his frown remained firmly in place.

“Julia, what on earth is going on? Have you completely lost your sense of reason, of decency? Oh my God! Look at your face!”

She winced at the outburst, she hated upsetting him and knew she had gone too far this time. She had known it from the moment Florence had begged to be accompanied, but she could not have turned her back on the girl, not even knowing it would cause her uncle so much upset.

“Please, sit, Uncle. You will understand once I explain.”

“Not this time, Julia. Not this time. I demand you come home immediately before a bad situation becomes irreversible.”

“I cannot, but it is not for any foolish reason. Please hear me out, I would not ask this of you unless it was important,” she pleaded with him.

He eventually sat in a chair, looking defeated and distraught. Julia crossed to him and crouched before him on the rug. “This is too much, Julia. I understand your need to protect others but to be in a gentleman’s home, and alone? And who on earth has hurt you? I knew you would be injured if you continued in this vein and now look at you!”

“Truly, it is not as it seems,” Julia started. She explained everything that had happened that evening, even with the first fight. She thought it was important to separate the fact that what had happened with Hugh was not the cause of her being injured. By the time she had reached the end, she had hoped that there would be some relief in her uncle's features, but he looked even more concerned.

"You cannot remain here," he said. "I understand you responding to a young girl's plea, but she is safe and protected now. You can leave without any pangs to that oversensitive conscience of yours."

"That is not so," Julia said. "She has clearly been raised outside of her social sphere and feels lost. I can help her; though our situations are different, the feelings are still the same."

"Oh, dear child, when will you ever let the past rest?" William almost begged of her. "It does not matter that I am in daily fear of you being injured or worse, that is largely irrelevant, but you are not living, Julia. You are clinging onto a past that has gone, and there is nothing you, I, or anyone else can do about it. How many times are we going to have this conversation? Until the day you are found lifeless?"

Julia stood. It was her time to pace the room, but eventually she stopped in front of the fire, letting the heat warm her still cold body. "I know what you say is true. I do, honestly. I just do not think I can ever let them go," she admitted for the first time. "I am afraid to even try to do it because without my cause I have no focus in my life, no aim, nothing. What would I do?"

"Just let yourself be a young woman, enjoy balls and dancing and flirting," William said.

"I am hardly a young woman, and how soon do you think it would be before I locked myself away if I had to attend entertainments every night of the week?" Julia asked dryly.

"At least allow yourself to get bored, allow yourself to live for the future and see what happens."

"I will try, I promise. But I cannot leave Florence yet, even though it puts my own reputation under threat, you must understand that I could not abandon her," Julia conceded.

William sighed. "In that case I will send for my portmanteau in addition to yours. I am sure his lordship has guest chambers enough to house me as well as you and his niece."

"You cannot stay here!" Julia was stunned at her uncle's solution, and she could only imagine what Hugh's response would be to find not only herself in residence, but also the uncle many mocked for his madcap inventions. She was realistic enough to know full well that he was considered eccentric at best and a comedy character at worse. For a top of the tree gentleman like Hugh, it would not be an acceptable arrangement, she was sure.

"If I cannot, neither can you. I will not be moved on this, Julia. I am to be your chaperone whilst you are under a single man's roof, and on this I will not be swayed, persuaded or cajoled like you usually use to get your own way."

"You make me sound like a spoiled brat!" Julia said in disgust.

"What is the saying? If the cap fits? I think you better stop this conversation; after all, I have conceded so much, there are limits to even my co-operation. I need to seek the assistance of the butler to send for our belongings. The sooner you are dressed in something more appropriate, the better."

Julia knew when to push something with her uncle, and this most definitely was not one of those times. She was still stinging that he thought her some spoiled child, so decided not to antagonise him any further. Opening the door, she indicated that the butler was needed and quickly explained to him that they needed provisions from her home.

"Of course, I shall have a room prepared."

"You are very good, aren't you?" Julia asked with a smile.

"I beg your pardon?" the butler responded.

"All that has happened tonight, you have taken in your stride. Either you are the most unflustered servant ever to be employed, or so many strange events have happened in this household that this is nothing to be surprised about," Julia said, being unusually frank with him.

The butler allowed himself a small smile. "A good servant never tells."

Julia laughed. "After this evening, I, for one, am certainly glad of that! We have not been formally introduced; I am Miss Julia Marsh, and this is my uncle, Mr William Marsh. It seems we are to be resident for a little while."

"It is a pleasure to make your acquaintance, and I am sure Miss Florence will appreciate you being here. I am Richards, Miss Marsh."

"It is not *her* reaction at our relocation here that I am concerned about," Julia said and was not reassured when the butler inclined his head but said nothing to soothe her concerns.

It was over two hours later that Julia finally fell into bed. She had checked on Hugh again, but there was no change. His valet was remaining with him, but he was unlikely to stir. There was no sign of fever as yet, which was a relief, but it was still very early to know if he would succumb to one. When she checked on Florence, Julia was glad to see that the girl was curled into a ball, fast asleep and looking restful. Julia hoped she would have only good dreams.

It was with stinging eyes and dismay that Julia realised that dawn was breaking before she closed the door on her own chamber. It was located next door to Florence, more credit to the foresight of Richards.

She took off her outer clothes, and instead of looking through the portmanteau which had been delivered from Half Moon Street, she just pulled back the covers of the bed and climbed in. Asleep within minutes, her dreams were filled with nightmares of not reaching Hugh in time.

Chapter 8

Julia awoke a lot later in the morning than she had intended and would have slept longer, only Florence knocked on her door.

When she mumbled a welcome, Florence peeped around the door. “Are you awake?”

“I am now,” Julia replied. “Come in.”

“I have had a bath and I feel wonderful!” Florence smiled at Julia.

“But what are you wearing?” Julia asked at the strange ensemble Florence was dressed in.

Florence laughed. “It was Richards’ idea. He said that there were some old clothes in the attic that might do for me until I could get some new ones. I think they wanted to burn the clothes I arrived in.”

Julia could understand that sentiment, they had been little more than rags. “I think perhaps Richards is not aware of how long those clothes have been stored away. You look like a ghost from a previous era.”

“I know! When I saw myself in the looking glass, I laughed like I had not done in years.” She sobered a little. “I still think this is all a dream. I stayed in the bath until the maid begged me to come out. She was afraid I would catch my death of cold, but it was such a relief to scrub my skin to try and get rid of the grime of the places I have been staying in."

"In that case, these clothes are wonderful. Anything which can make you feel good about yourself is worth wearing."

"I do look ridiculous though."

"Perhaps a little." Julia smiled. "There are plenty of modistes who will happily visit the house and measure you for a new wardrobe."

"I need to wait until my uncle agrees to spending some money on me. He might not want to."

"I doubt he will raise any arguments," Julia responded, climbing out of bed.

"Does your face hurt much? It looks painful," Florence said.

Julia peered in her looking glass; a large purple bruise covered her cheekbone and around her eye. She was lucky that although somewhat swollen, she could still see quite well, only her eyelid drooped a little. "It looks worse than it is," she said.

"I am sorry you were hurt."

Julia decided not to go into details about what had happened before she had reached Florence and Hugh, life was complicated enough. "Let me get dressed and we can go and check on your uncle. I have to tell you that my own uncle has joined us last night and will be staying whilst I am here."

"Oh, Uncle William? I have already met him, we had breakfast together. He's delightful and has been telling me all about his inventions. I told him that he needs to invent more for young women to protect themselves against blaggards. He said I reminded him of you," Florence said, more than happy with the comparison.

***

Julia had correctly predicted Hugh's response when he saw his niece. He was sat up in bed when they were allowed into his room. Although he looked pale, Julia was relieved to see his features were not flushed and he was bright-eyed. She hoped that outwardly she carried herself with some modicum of detachment, for her insides jolted at the sight of Hugh in only his nightshirt. He looked younger, and with his dark hair still ruffled from sleep, she felt an even greater pull to him than she had already. She found it mildly annoying that he was handsome both when he was dressed to perfection and when he was dishevelled.

Trying to get her feelings back into some sort of order, she concentrated on checking for signs that he was not ill. Feeling she could breathe easier once she had seen him looking as well as could be expected, her relief soon turned to amusement when Hugh saw Florence and his welcoming smile turned to a look of horror.

"What the devil are you wearing, child?" he demanded, unapologetic for his language.

Florence grinned. "Miss Marsh thought you would be horrified."

"Then Miss Marsh is quite correct," Hugh responded.

"I have taken it upon myself to seek Richards' help to send for a modiste to visit as soon as was possible. I have recommended my own," Julia said.

"I thank you for your forethought, and I can only be grateful that I am not allowed out of this bed for some time, for I certainly would not be leaving this house with Florence on my arm dressed in such a fashion. Long lost niece or not," Hugh said, almost shuddering at the thought.

"It would certainly be one way to launch her that society would not forget in a hurry," Julia said.

"Launch me into society? No! I can't do that!" Florence said, all good humour gone.

"Florence, until I marry and produce an heir, which I have no intention of doing, you are the heir to the Bryn estate. The title will go to some other relative, but the estate which is not entailed will go to you as you are the next in line," Hugh said. "Of course you need to take your place in society."

"But I don't know what to do! I will embarrass myself and be the laughing stock. Ma told me how cruel society could be."

Julia saw a flash of pain cross Hugh's features and could understand it, he had lost his sister and she knew what loss felt like. She turned to Florence. "I am sure your uncle will allow you time to learn what you need to know and to become accustomed to your new situation. There is plenty of time before you need to be bored to tears at yet another ball or theatre show."

Florence smiled a little, still clearly unsure and afraid. "I would not mind going to the theatre," she admitted.

"We can do that long before you are launched in society; we do not need to sit in a box and attract attention to ourselves," Julia said.

"You sound like you dislike attention, Miss Marsh," Hugh drawled. "But I am afraid you have my full attention when you have so clearly been injured. How did that happen?"

"I am an expert at blending into the background, it is usually the best place to be, but sometimes people do not take good advice, and I am afraid I was a little overconfident in my abilities." She saw a flicker of something pass over his face, but he schooled his features into their usual bland expression before she could interpret the meaning. One thing was certain, she was convinced this was a topic which would be raised again between them.

"I believe I have another guest in my house, one who seems to have blended in as he has not been to see me thus far," Hugh said. "It is clearly a family talent."

Julia flushed. "The choice was that he stay, or I return to Half Moon Street. I had no option but to agree to his company if I was to help Miss Weston until you are well enough to take over."

"Then he shall be welcomed," Hugh said magnanimously. "Although I hope he does not take over my study as his workshop."

"If you take too long to recover that could be a serious possibility, but for now your study is safe," Julia said, glad he had lightened his tone. She had dreaded raising the subject of her uncle, but it seemed Hugh was aware of everything that was going on, even though he was confined to bed.

"In that case, I will do as the doctor bids, but I hope you two will not abandon me completely," Hugh said. "York, here, is not much company."

The valet's expression did not flicker, but Julia came to his defence. "If you abuse the member of staff who has stayed up all night to make sure you were tended to, then you can certainly remain alone and bored, my lord," she said stiffly.

Hugh looked at York with a pained expression. "And I thought the company of Miss Marsh would be preferable to yours. I beg your pardon, York. You are by far the more appealing companion. Forgive my presumption."

"You are a beast," Julia responded, scowling when she received a delighted smile at her words. "I think it is time to leave your uncle be, Miss Weston. It is obvious he is tiring for he is even more crotchety than usual."

Florence had watched the exchange with wonder, and dutifully followed Julia out of the room. "You aren't afraid of him in the slightest, are you?" she asked as they returned downstairs.

"Afraid of him? Why on earth would I be?" Julia asked in genuine surprise.

"He is an earl. Ma told me how cruel her father was and what he would do to her if he considered she misbehaved. She once got locked in her chamber for a day for refusing to mount the horse her father demanded she ride. She said it was the meanest in the stables, and he wanted her to fall off it to build her character. He said it would do her the world of good."

"It could have killed her," Julia said.

"Yes, that was what she was afraid of. He locked her away and didn't allow any of the staff to give her anything to eat until she agreed to go on the horse," Florence continued.

"And I suppose she gave in eventually or risked starving to death."

"Yes, and she fell badly. Her father walked away muttering that she was a worthless girl, and he hoped to god she was his only one. She never sat on another horse," Florence said.

"Those actions were not the actions of an earl," Julia said gently. "They were the actions of a cruel man; he could have been an innkeeper or a duke, he would have still been cruel."

"I did sometimes wish we could go to the family home, though, when we were really hungry and cold," Florence admitted. "Ma did all she could, but sometimes there was nothing else she could do apart from sell herself, which she refused to do, and I am glad that she did not sink so low."

Julia stopped at the bottom of the stairs and embraced Florence. The child folded into her arms as if she had not had many reassuring embraces, probably never since her mother died, Julia thought. "She sounds like a strong woman who was determined to do the best she could in the worst circumstances. From the little you have said about your grandfather, I doubt she would have received a welcome if she had returned home."

"That's what she used to say," Florence said, still clinging to Julia. "She made me promise not to seek them out no matter how bad things got."

Julia moved so she could look at Florence. "I understand why she said that and I cannot claim to know your uncle well, but he has obviously gone to a lot of trouble, and though his nature is brusque, I do not believe he is a cruel man. If he had been, he would not have walked the streets of London seeking you. Those are not the streets that anyone would willingly choose to wander around."

"What were you doing there? You are a gentlewoman, yet you were dressed in men's clothes. I have puzzled about it all morning and your uncle would not give anything away," Florence said.

"I will tell you one day, but if I do not get my breakfast soon, I will be fainting on the spot," Julia said, delaying for time. She was not yet sure what to reveal to Florence. The girl was intelligent, but the more people knew about what she did, the more at risk she was of being revealed as the shadow. Accepting that she would have to take whatever society decided to punish her with if that happened was one thing, but causing her uncle to lose his sponsors, of which he had few enough already, was something she would not risk.

Chapter 9

Hugh flopped back on his pillows when Julia and Florence had left and looked at his valet with a pained expression. "I think having a niece about the place is going to cause more trouble and effort than I had anticipated. Especially as she has adopted a termagant as her ally." The valet gave no response, and Hugh sighed dramatically. "Am I to be deserted by my staff now there is a defender of their rights in the house?"

"Quite possibly."

"Damn you," Hugh said good-naturedly. "The chit has some sort of saviour complex; she needs to be doing good all the time."

"That is a commendable use of her time, many would say," the valet responded.

"Not if it constantly puts her at risk and in danger. Although I suppose I was the one who did not avoid the knife," Hugh said with derision. His words hid the fact that he was raging inside at the unknown person who had hurt her. Seeing her injury, the side of her face almost covered in a bruise had him wanting to leave his bed and damn the consequences. His fists had clenched; he would kill the damned cur if he ever got hold of him.

The valet left the room and Hugh stared at the canopy of his bed, pondering over what he could remember of the night he had found Florence. He had been terrified that the men were going to overpower him, and if that had happened, Florence would have been at their mercy.

When he had found her after all that searching, it had felt like a weight had been lifted from his shoulders, and it had nothing to do with finding the heir to his fortune. It was about righting a wrong, but he would never admit that to anyone, he was too ashamed that his parents had acted the way they had. Yes, his mother could not have changed his father's mind, but she could have found some way to help her only daughter. Those thoughts had tainted his relationship with his mother, and he thought she had known it for she had never seemed comfortable in his presence.

As for his father, he hoped he rotted in hell for what he had done. Florence had spent so much time alone and unprotected, he went cold at the thought of what could have happened to her. For God's sake, he cursed, even now he did not know what had gone on in her past, she could already have been ruined.

He hated the thought, but he refused to condemn her or punish her if she was. He was not his father and would not make the mistakes and unfair decisions his father had. Survival on the streets was hard, she would have a better life from now on, and he would make sure she married someone who deserved her and who would treat her with kindness. That was all that was important.

Julia. Now there was someone else he could not stop thinking about. When another had joined the fight, he had known instinctively that it was her. Half terrified for her but more grateful for her help, it had spurred him on to try to finish the fight, so she would not get hurt. He had failed, for the bruising around her face looked painful. He went cold at the thought that she might have been the one who was stabbed.

He should have noticed the man was armed. The situation was that another inch or two and he would have been killed instantly and in no position to help anyone. The thought made him shudder. Why the heck could she not stay out of harm's way, blast her?

He was interrupted from his musings by the announcement that John had arrived to see him. "Show him in," he instructed Richards, and within moments his friend joined him.

"How the devil are you? I am thankful that I am not visiting a corpse today as I have always feared, but it seems you had some help last night," John said, walking in and throwing a copy of a newspaper on the bed. "You are famous, my friend. Apparently the shadow saved you and a young lady from attack last night. I presume they were not talking about the delectable Kathryn?"

"Good God, no!" Hugh said. "I finally found my niece."

"Really? Now that is news indeed. Tell me all, especially the bit about you needing to be rescued," John said, sitting in a chair and crossing his ankles. "Everyone is going to want to spar with you the next time you venture into the club, now the news is out that you could not fight off an attacker."

"There were three!" Hugh insisted. "You blasted coxcomb! You have just come in here to annoy me while I cannot retaliate by boxing your ears for your impertinence, have you not?"

"Of course." John smiled, no longer worried about his friend now he had seen him. "Do you think me a fool to miss such an opportunity? I do insist that you reveal exactly what happened, though."

Hugh told him of the attack and what had happened since. He glossed over the fact that Julia and her uncle were now staying with him because of Florence, but John was not the type of friend to let a brief comment that Hugh made pass so easily.

"Miss Marsh the bluestocking is staying under your roof? With the mad inventor? I hope you have ordered new windows and doors for he will likely blow them off," John laughed.

“I think the roof would be in more danger, as the attics are the only place where there is space to experiment,” Julia said as she walked into the room, carrying a tray. “I thought I would bring you some of the broth, which Cook has made especially for you,” she said to Hugh.

“A maid could have brought that,” Hugh said, glaring at his friend.

“As we are causing more work for your servants, it is only fair we help when we can.”

“I beg your pardon, Miss Marsh,” John said, flushing red and noticing the look of fury Hugh was aiming in his direction.

“What for? Claiming that I am a bluestocking, which everyone knows I am, or suggesting that my uncle is in danger of damaging his lordship’s house? He probably is, of which I have warned our host. There is no point in apologising for speaking the truth.”

John was mortified further and looked down like some naughty schoolboy until Julia had placed the tray on the bed and stepped back. “Richards is going to bring a decanter up. Good morning to you, gentlemen,” Julia said before leaving the room.

“Oh Lord!” John moaned when the door clicked shut behind Julia. “I did not think I could feel any worse and now I know I can. And what on earth has she done to her face?”

"That is none of your concern! What the deuce possessed you to speak in such a careless way?" Hugh demanded. "I would have expected it of me, but you are supposed to be the decent one of the two of us."

"I think I got overexcited at the thought of you needing to be rescued and then hearing who your guests were. I am truly sorry."

"It is not I you should be begging forgiveness of," Hugh said. "I hope you have deep pockets, for I feel you are going to be spending a lot on fripperies to try and convince Miss Marsh that you aren't the ninnyhammer she must think you are."

"I will do anything."

"Good. Start by not insulting the woman who is helping my niece to settle in to a strange new world, for after seeing her once this morning, I am convinced that I am certainly not up to the task."

John smiled, relieved that the subject had changed from his blunder. "In that case, I will watch with interest. Am I to meet her?"

"Not yet," Hugh said. "She is a little overwhelmed at the moment, but I am sure she will soon come about as she has spirit, also Richards went into the attics and found some clothes from centuries ago by the looks of them. You will meet her when she feels more comfortable and looks presentable, believe me the horror of that clothing is not to be underestimated."

"I am glad you found her," John said.

"So am I, but when I thought the hard thing was finding her, I was being a naïve fool. I have a feeling my life has changed forever."

"And is that a bad thing?" John asked.

"With Florence in my life, it most certainly is not," Hugh said. He did not admit that the thought of being in daily, close contact with Julia was also something he was looking forward to more than he had thought possible. Never before had any female breached his home, but here she was and he was happy about it, even anticipating their time together.

Yes, it seemed within one day, his life had changed completely, and for the first time in his life, he was looking forward to the future.

***

Hugh might have been considered with some suspicion by William, but one of his actions met with his wholehearted approval. He managed to persuade Julia not to go back onto the streets at night for the foreseeable future at least. His request was made during a conversation that took place on their first afternoon together, two days after the attack had happened. Florence had decided to have another bath, and William was reading something interesting he had discovered in Hugh's study, so Julia had taken up some tea and sat with Hugh for a while.

She had been looking for a reason to see him. Yes, she popped in regularly to check on him, but there was usually someone else there and she felt embarrassed about intruding into his bedchamber. That morning though he had left his bed and moved to his own private sitting room.

Julia met the valet on the stairs, carrying a tray. "Are you taking that to his lordship?" she asked.

"Yes, miss. Cook is determined to build up his strength in the form of serving tea and cakes every hour between meals."

"He will be needing a new wardrobe if he eats everything she sends up," Julia laughed.

"Quite so," York responded with a twinkle in his eyes.

"Let me take it, and I will help demolish these lovely fancies," Julia said, reaching for the tray. "I need to speak to him about Miss Weston anyway."

"I am sure he will appreciate the help with the cakes," York said, handing the tray over.

She kicked the bottom of the door with her foot as she entered the room next to the master bedchamber. Hugh looked up in surprise at the sound and sudden lurch of the door.

"Do not ever go into service, Miss Marsh," he said drolly. "I fear you would be cast off within the day."

"How rude! When I have specifically come in to help you eat this feast," Julia said, placing the heavy tray at the table closest to Hugh. It was a masculine room but tastefully decorated in blues. Overlooking the drive, it was a perfect position should one wish to seek refuge but continue to be aware of the comings and goings of the house.

"In that case, please take a seat. Any help is gratefully received, I do not think I shall ever eat cake again when I am back up and about."

"What nonsense you speak!" Julia said. "Who could ever tire of cake?"

"I never thought I would, but believe me after these few days, just the thought of them turns my stomach."

"Talking of which, you are looking more rotund since I last saw you," she lied.

"Wretch!" Hugh laughed at her. "I am glad you are here, though. I want to discuss your night-time adventures."

Julia rolled her eyes, but listened as he explained that he would wish her not to go out while she was tutoring Florence. "There is just too much at risk for us all," he finished, conscious that his reasoning was not being accepted. She would not agree to his request easily, he was fully aware of that.

"You want me to stop helping people in danger just because you need someone to prepare your niece for society? I think that is a very unworthy reason to give up doing the good I can do by venturing out, as much as I like Florence." Julia and Florence had quickly agreed that formalities were unnecessary and were using their given names.

"Her reputation is so fragile and will be for some time, I cannot risk you being discovered and associated with her. For myself, it would not affect my reputation."

"It could enhance it," Julia retorted. Hugh raised his eyebrows at her but made no comment. "I know I am old enough to act the chaperone, but I really think you need someone who can introduce her to the right people. I will not be able to obtain tickets for Almack's or anything of the kind. I do not socialise in the highest circles, my lord, you already know that."

"Oh blast! I am going to have to spend a dreary night there, aren't I? Damn my father a thousand times."

Julia laughed. "Being a hero is harder than you imagined."

"I am no hero, you wear that crown with what you have done," Hugh said. "I was just righting a wrong, but I did not think of the implications of my actions beyond finding Florence."

"I certainly do not wear the crown of hero," Julia said heatedly. "I, too, am just trying to right something. I cannot affect the situation I would like to, but I can help others."

Hugh decided to change tack a little. "Florence seems very young, even for her sixteen years."

"Yes, she does."

"There is no point sending her to the schoolroom for a year. She needs to be with someone she trusts and who has the patience to teach her the practical side of being a young woman in society."

Julia narrowed her eyes at him. "Have you been speaking to Florence?"

"No," Hugh answered honestly. "The thought of conversation with her terrifies me a little, but I hope that will improve when she does not offend my eyes every time she enters the room. I hope your modiste works quickly."

"You are horrible," Julia said.

"Oh, most definitely. It has been said on more than one occasion."

"Let me guess, by your mistresses. Like the one you were clearly trying to rid yourself of when we danced."

He did not hide the fury he felt at her inappropriate comment. "You have no right to know about such things!"

Julia smiled, completely unaffected by his rage. "The advantage of being on the edges of society is that you get to watch what is going on without people realising what they are giving away. It is fascinating and highly entertaining."

"In that case, you should know that my so-called mistress was seeing someone else, and I refuse to be treated the fool," he said defensively.

"Was she really? How very wicked of her."

"You are a strange creature. Are you not at least a little shocked?" Hugh seemed genuinely curious and a little overwhelmed at the turn the conversation had taken.

"Should I be?" Julia asked in mock innocence.

"I should probably throw you out of my house for not being horrified, for surely a true gentlewoman would be."

"Oh, that is a wonderful idea! Please throw us out and then I can carry on as if we had never met."

"That, Miss Marsh, is never going to happen. You are in my life now and I am thankful for it. You cannot avoid me no matter how hard you might wish to. I will follow you around if you try to disassociate yourself from us and, believe me, I do not give up easily."

A silence descended between them as if they were both waiting for the other to speak. Julia was flustered at the comment he had made, it had felt as if there was more meaning behind the words.

Whilst Julia was trying to work out what Hugh really meant by his cryptic words, he was worried that he had said too much. He watched Julia closely; was she going to reject him? For if she mocked him or gave him a set-down, it would certainly feel like a rejection, and for some reason, he really wanted her to agree and remain with him. He tried to convince himself that it was for Florence's benefit, but even to his own mind, his thoughts were unconvincing.

Julia was the one to break the silence. "It really would not do for me to be found out while I am spending time with Florence. I cannot say that I agree with giving up going out in the evenings, but I will stop it until she is in a position where my assistance is no longer needed. You do need to look for a more permanent chaperone, though. I cannot commit to Florence forever, as much as I like her."

"I can pay you for your services," Hugh said quickly.

"That is not necessary," came the stiff response.

"I do not mean to insult you, but you must let me compensate you in some way."

Julia grinned. “Watching you bring out your niece and being forced to play the pretty with all the hostesses will be all the payment I need.”

“Oh Lord!”

“Have you considered the looks or comments which could be made when Florence is introduced as Miss Weston?” Julia asked. “Her mother having not been married will risk her being accepted into society at all.”

Hugh nodded in agreement. “I have considered that and will make it known that Florence has decided to take on the family name at my request. It is not a perfect solution, but everyone knows how I can be so they will not be surprised at my request.”

Julia raised her eyebrows in amusement. “Sometimes being known as an ogre can come in useful.”

“Exactly. I will also acknowledge that we have discovered some distant relative who joins our two families, so I asked for your help in my hour of need.”

“Be assured I will be with you every step of the way, but I do have my own life to live and I am not willing to be Florence’s chaperone until she marries; that could be years off.”

“Of course. I hope it is, for as much as I am unprepared for all this, I do not wish her to leave immediately; we have a lot of time to make up for. I will find someone who can take over the role when

Florence is more settled. Thank you, I really do appreciate it," Hugh said.

"I should jolly well hope so, and it will put Uncle William's mind at rest. I think my trips out have been very trying for him."

"I am not surprised. I have only known you a short while and your antics have given me the shivers on more than one occasion."

"With that knowledge, I am almost tempted to continue." Julia grinned at him.

"You, Miss Marsh, have surely been sent to torment my previously peaceful life."

"I do hope so."

Chapter 10

"Miss Marsh, there is a Miss Holmes wishing to know if you are at home," Richards said two days later, while Julia was with Florence in the drawing room practising needlework.

"Grace? How on earth has she tracked me here?" Julia gasped. She could say she was not at home, but Grace would know she was avoiding her, which would be correct, but to see her would start a conversation that Julia was not sure she could have with her friend.

She sighed, there was no point hiding from Grace as she had missed the club meeting that she had promised to attend. The fact that her face still sported a purple bruise had meant that she could not go to the eagerly anticipated event, there would have been far too many questions from her friends.

"I will see her in the morning room," she said to Richards. Turning to Florence, she smiled. "Grace is a good friend and I would like you to meet her as soon as it is pertinent, but I think for now you should remain here and carry on with your work."

"I would feel happier to meet your friends when I look more presentable," Florence said, glancing at her dress. The modiste was working hard, but as yet she had no more appropriate clothes.

Julia smiled. "Grace would definitely find your attire amusing. Please excuse me, I hope I will not be too long."

Walking down the stairs, she tried to work out what she would say to convince Grace of what had happened and decided that something as near to the truth as she could risk would be the safest option.

Entering the morning room, Julia held out her hands to her friend. "How lovely to see you! Did you visit Half Moon Street and they told you we were here?" she asked.

"I was worried about you, and from the look of you, it seems I was right to be so," Grace said, kissing Julia's uninjured cheek and gently pulling her to sit next to her on a sofa. "You forget that my lady's maid is your cook's sister, so news between the households travels fast. Especially something as scandalous as this." She gently touched Julia's face. The action was done in a maternal way, almost as if she wished she could wipe away the bruising.

"There is nothing scandalous about taking a punch to the face, I can assure you," Julia responded.

"Oh Julia, what have you been up to and what on earth happened that you are now living with the

Earl of Bryn? That is a development I could never have foreseen."

Julia laughed. "Nor I. Let me ring for some tea first, then I can tell you the whole sorry tale."

Richards soon entered with a tray, clearly having anticipated the request, and Julia busied herself with pouring the tea. "I was sorry to have missed the talk. Was Caroline Herschel interesting?"

"She was fascinating, as you would imagine. The girls had a good night and are hoping she will come back one day, but she does travel around a lot. Your presence was missed."

"I am sorry. I had every intention of going, but when this happened—" she touched her face "—I just could not face the questions. I will be hiding away until the bruising can no longer be seen. I never thought I was vain, but it seems I do possess some vanity after all."

"I have the suspicion it would be answering the questions that would keep you away more than how you looked," Grace said, taking a sip of her tea but never looking away from Julia.

"Well, yes, but you can understand that having been part of a robbery, I would not wish to talk about it."

"The robbery was reported to involve Lord Bryn and a young lady. One young lady. I believe he has found his long searched for niece that night," Grace said.

"I really need to have a word with Cook," Julia muttered. "Is there no loyalty from staff these days?"

"Let me just say that I have heard a few things about you, Julia, that did not quite add up until recently. But I think the events of the last few days has meant that some of my confusion has been lifted," Grace said. Her tone was light and friendly as it always was, but there was almost the hint that Julia should not treat her like a fool, though the woman would never utter such words.

"What things have you heard?"

"I suppose I should have said heard and seen," Grace clarified. "We have been friends for years now, and I sometimes feel like the matriarch of the group as I am twenty years older than the rest of you, but you are the one who has always worried me."

"Why? You never said anything," Julia said. She felt that yet another person was about to know her secrets and although part of her wanted to just tell Grace and get it over with, the other part of her hoped in vain that Grace might not have made the link.

"Arabella has to bear with her physical scars," she said of another member of the Bluestocking Club who had virtually become a recluse after a carriage accident. "But with you, your scars could not be seen, but they affected you as much as Arabella's have impacted her. She has hidden herself away, but with you it was different; you had to help those in need, especially those in danger."

Julia flopped back against the cushioned seat. "How long have you known?"

"A while. I heard about you going out at night. You did not seriously believe that servants would not know that you were leaving and returning through their entrance, did you?"

"Clearly I did," Julia huffed. "More fool me."

"The clothing did not make sense until the newspapers started to describe the shadow," Grace said, her tone gentler. "You have been putting yourself at such a risk dressing and acting as a man, although some would say that you would be even more at risk if you had been discovered as a young, innocent woman."

"I know, but I could not see any other way to help those in need."

"Did your uncle know?"

"He did and has done everything he could to dissuade me. He eventually started to invent protections for me in the hope that if I would not stop, I could at least fight people off. It did not always work."

"And I am presuming you are the female the women of the *ton* are talking about who has had lessons from Gentleman Jackson and Mr Angelo?"

"Oh fiddlesticks! Does everyone know?" Julia moaned, covering her face with her hands.

"The men know about your lessons, but no one has revealed who you are. I think it is more that they do not know rather than they are keeping a secret. What about Lord Bryn?"

"Yes, he found out one night while searching for his niece. He has persuaded me to stop for the moment as I am helping his niece until he finds a suitable companion for her."

"That is something at least. I have been reading the papers every morning with the dread of seeing that you were seriously injured or worse."

"Most of those stories were not of me," Julia said.

"I supposed not when you were at a ball one evening, and in the morning there was another report. Either there were more people copying you, or you had boundless energy."

"I wish I had," Julia said. "Can I be honest with you?"

"I would appreciate that very much."

"I did not know how to stop. Oh, I have been all bravado and determination, and I still believe I should be doing something to help, but there were a couple of instances that scared me and brought it home that I was not infallible. I had come to the conclusion that I was going to end the exact way my parents had, stabbed and left to die."

"Oh, Julia, my sweet child. Why did you not come to me?" Grace asked, pained to know her friend had been suffering and none of their group had known to what extent.

"I did not want to appear cowardly. His lordship has given me the perfect way out and I argued with him about it. How ridiculous am I to have done that? I should have thanked him for giving me the excuse I needed to stop," Julia said. Tears were pouring down her cheeks, but she brushed them away angrily.

"He might be known as a rake and a cad, but I will always look more favourably on him for that reason alone," Grace said, handing Julia a handkerchief, without making comment about the tears.

Julia hiccupped a laugh. "I do not think he is a completely reformed character."

"Ah, rakes usually need the guidance of a good woman," Grace said with a smile, which turned into a laugh at Julia's expression. "Do not roast me, I just want to see all of my girls happy. At least now I can rest easy knowing you are not roaming the streets at night."

"I am ashamed at how many people I have worried," Julia said honestly.

"It was your quest, but now it is time to look to the future, not the past."

"That is what Uncle William has said on more than one occasion."

"For the first time in my life, I agree with him," Grace said. "And those are words I never thought that I would utter."

"Please do not tell the others," Julia begged, missing the slight flush that had tinged Grace's cheeks when speaking about William.

"I promise they will hear nothing from me," Grace assured her. "Now tell me all about this niece you are looking after."

Julia was grateful for the change of subject, and the two women chatted for another half-hour before Grace stood to leave.

"If you need anything at all, you just let me know, and as soon as that bruising goes, I expect to see you at the club with young Florence," Grace said, embracing Julia.

"She might be bored, you know how we ramble on," Julia said.

"She has survived in a cruel world on only her wits, she is clearly an intelligent girl, I know that without meeting her. I am sure she will be a diamond of the season when she finally makes her come out, but until then we can give her company that she just might enjoy," Grace said.

"Thank you."

"Anything for my girls," Grace said, and with a last kiss on the cheek, she let Richards lead her out.

Julia sat back down once she heard the front door close; she needed a moment to gather her thoughts before returning to Florence. She had suspected Grace thought something was amiss with her, but she would never have guessed that she knew so much. Nor had she realised that the servants knew about her exploits either! She had been foolishly single-minded and that had to stop.

In her heart she knew it had stopped already. She had been speaking the truth when she said she had wanted an excuse to stop but had not known how to find one. Hugh had offered her that and he could never know how grateful she was.

Hugh. He was all she had thought of these past weeks, and wanting to spend time with him was probably a large part of her change in heart. He had got under her skin from the first moment he had burst into her life. Was he to be her future? He had hinted he would be, but without him being completely frank with his words, she doubted the meaning of what he had said.

She could not presume so much, as those could have been words said purely to get his own way. He was a taciturn man of the world, and she was a spinster bluestocking. He would probably laugh at the thought of her even considering a future with him. No, she would just have to admire from afar and try to accept that they would be nothing other than friends.

Her thoughts were disturbed by Richards. “Miss Marsh, I apologise for disturbing you, but his lordship says that if you do not rescue him from Miss Florence trying to teach him embroidery, he is going to leave the house immediately.”

Julia laughed, all melancholy thoughts forgotten. “I suppose I should rescue him, but I am tempted to let him suffer for a little while,” she said.

“It has been ten minutes since he issued his second request,” Richards said with a betraying twinkle in his eyes. “I thought an appropriate amount of time had passed and it was time to inform you.”

“I think you are probably right.” Julia smiled back at the butler. “I do hope he has given in and we find him with needle and thread in his hands.”

“From what I could see of Miss Florence’s determination, it would not surprise me in the least,” Richards responded.

“Excellent!”

Chapter 11

Disappointingly, Hugh was not found brandishing a needle, but the incident was the catalyst in his returning downstairs. He walked slower than normal and moved around more gingerly, but he claimed to be perfectly well, refusing to remain ensconced in his suite of rooms any longer.

Florence and Julia were working all day and every day on the basic skills needed to be an acceptable member of the *ton*. Florence had complained on more than one occasion that most of it was boring her half to death.

"What does it matter if I can sew letters on a handkerchief?" she moaned, sucking the blood from her finger for the second time in as many minutes.

"You might want to give one to a beau," Hugh said. He was reading the paper in the morning room, an instance which was becoming a habit.

"Pfftt! Who is going to want me?" Florence said. "I too easily fall back into speaking like I just came out of the gutter, which I have, and if I do that when in company, I am likely to be condemned as the interloper that I am."

"You are an heiress, you will be sought after," Hugh dismissed her concerns.

"I beg to differ," Julia said as she leaned over and helped Florence with the difficult embroidery stitch.

Hugh crumpled the paper as he looked at Julia. "Although I do not wish for Florence to secure one, we both know that there are fortune hunters enough who would accept anything to get their hands on a steady supply of blunt."

"You old romantic, you," Julia responded. "Thankfully, Florence will have your support, which will protect her when those types start sniffing around. They are the worst kind but can be quite vindictive when you offer a set-down, so just be careful around them," she warned Florence.

"You sound as if you have had to deal with them," Florence said.

"Oh yes, anyone with an inheritance will attract them."

"How did you set them down carefully?"

"I did not care what they did to me or my reputation, so I told them exactly what I thought of their antics," Julia replied with a grin.

Hugh let out a crack of laughter. "Why am I not surprised? I am just astounded that your reputation of being a termagant has not reached me earlier."

"I do not attend, or did not attend," Julia corrected herself quickly, "many of the entertainments. I had other things I wanted to do instead."

"I wish I could avoid the balls," Florence moaned.

"Oh no! You are so young and pretty, you need to go out and explore society, have flirtations and enjoy dancing without concern about the past. Just concentrate on the future and you will have a good time," Julia said.

"You make it sound so easy, yet it seems harder than living the way I have been doing," Florence said.

"I am not saying it will all be plain sailing, but you have an uncle behind you to protect and support you when you need it."

"Like you did with Uncle William," Florence said. She had started to call him the familial title from the moment they had met, and William seemed as pleased to have inherited a niece, just as much as Florence was to have a second uncle.

"Yes. He was there when I needed him most and I will always thank him for that," Julia said, clearly uncomfortable with how the conversation had turned to her.

"He looks on you as the daughter he did not have," Florence said.

"I know. Now enough of this seriousness, we have a dance master's lesson to prepare for," Julia said. "I suggest you change into your dancing shoes before he arrives."

"Can you not accompany me?" Florence pleaded.

"No. You will have to do some things alone," Julia said. "He has been chosen for he is the best and the most patient; you will enjoy it, I promise. And if I am not there, I cannot see your mistakes."

Florence smiled. "There are going to be many of those."

"I will join you when my toes are safe from injury," Julia said to Florence's retreating form.

"I think she capitulated so easily because she hates sewing so much," Hugh said, finally putting his crumpled newspaper down.

"Most certainly," Julia agreed. "I am not very neat, but she makes my work look impressive. I hope with time and patience she will improve."

"I think she takes after me for being impatient," Hugh admitted. "I can see the family personality traits coming out as she settles in."

"Then the poor child is doomed."

Hugh laughed. "Probably. How long have you lived with your uncle?"

"Twelve years," Julia answered but stood up. "If you will excuse me, I have promised to visit my friend Grace as soon as it was practicable, and as Florence is engaged for the next few hours, it is a perfect opportunity."

"Of course," Hugh said. He was disappointed that he had lived with the woman for well over a week now, and still she tried to avoid any conversation which revealed anything about her background. Women usually fawned over him, telling him anything and everything to try to capture his attention, but she actively disliked answering questions about herself.

He watched the door close before picking up the newspaper once more, trying not to dwell on the fact that the next few hours would drag until the elusive Miss Marsh returned home.

***

Hugh was to have an unlooked-for opportunity to find out more when Julia sent a message to say she would be joining Grace for lunch and would return afterwards, and Florence decided that dancing was exhausting and would have a light lunch in her chamber before having a nap.

Thus, Hugh and William were alone in the dining room. Managing to force himself not to ask any personal questions until the servants had left them, he contented himself with letting William babble about the creation he was working on.

It had come as a surprise to Hugh that he actually liked William. Oh, he was forgetful and so completely absorbed in what he was doing that he would miss meals unless someone was sent to fetch him and remained with him until he admitted defeat and left whatever he was engrossed in, but he was an interesting man. He had travelled the world and had an outlook which was to question, rather than accept, which was refreshing.

Nodding to the footmen that their duties were at an end, Hugh stretched his legs under the table. He was determined that nothing would stop him from finding out more about Julia, so when a natural pause in William's chatter occurred, he got straight to the point.

"It must have been hard taking on a young woman as a single man. I feel we have a lot in common with our nieces now being under our care," he said.

"Even if I had not wished to do it, which I did, there was no one else who she could have gone to. It was hard that Julia had lost both her parents and was grieving badly, and I had lost a brother and sister-in-law whilst gaining a niece who I loved but had no idea how to comfort or help," William explained.

"I completely understand. I have not questioned Florence too much about her past because I do not know how I will deal with what she reveals. I imagine I will want to kill anyone who has tried to harm her."

William smiled. "Yes, I know that feeling. Every time Julia went out at night, I made her tell me what had happened more for her sake than mine. What she revealed would have me staring at my bed canopy long into the night because I am not like you, sir, I am no fighter, but I thought if she spoke about it, the experiences might not trouble her so much. They worried me beyond anything I have ever experienced, even when travelling, but it was all I could do to help. I would have liked to go out and punish those who challenged her, but I would have been a laughing stock."

"As I ended up injured in the last fight I had, I am reassessing my own capabilities in that department," Hugh said dryly. "How did your brother and his wife die?"

"It was an unfortunate circumstance," William said. "They had been on a night out, and we will never know why they chose to dismiss their coach and walk home. It had never happened before and still does not make sense. There was a witness who said they were set upon by a gang who demanded their valuables, which they gave, but my foolish brother thought he would be clever and did not hand over everything, probably not expecting the gang would search them. When they found a roll of notes, he was stabbed in cold blood, and my sister-in-law attacked the man who had stabbed Harold. You can guess they showed no compunction in treating her in the same way as they had my brother. The blaggards could have spared her; she reacted as anyone would have done in the situation, out of instinct rather than thinking her actions through."

"Good grief, they showed no mercy?" Hugh said, sickened. But it was not only with regards to Julia's parents that he felt so. It was also that for so long Julia had been in the same streets, alone, with the type of men who found it acceptable to kill a defenceless woman.

"No. The witness told the story but claimed she could not identify any of the gang. She was probably protecting herself, which I cannot blame her for. Putting her at risk would not bring Harold or Sarah back."

"It has clearly affected your niece deeply."

"She has had a good group of friends who have supported her, but it was almost as if she withdrew into herself after it happened. She has held herself back so much that I have given up hope of her ever finding someone who she can completely be herself with."

Hugh stopped himself from saying that she was herself with him. She clearly was not as she avoided mentioning any personal revelations. He paused when the thought struck him that he should not feel so concerned and discontent that she did not confide in him. She barely knew him; why would she trust him, especially with his reputation? The realisation deepened his frown and made his insides feel heavy.

"Yet she mentioned that she was an heiress," Hugh said. "I am surprised she is not wed."

"She blames it on being a bluestocking that she never married, but I think it is more that she will not allow herself to care for someone. I think she is afraid of losing them as she lost her parents."

"For someone who spends his time over a workbench, you seem to be very insightful," Hugh said.

"I like knowing what makes an object work, and that includes people, although I have had only a little luck in my levels of understanding where people are concerned," William admitted with a chuckle.

"Is that why you never married?"

"There was someone once," William explained. "But it is in the past and there is no use repining over what could have been. At least I have been fortunate enough to feel what it is like to love, I hold on to that."

"I can categorically say you have the advantage over me in that regard."

"That is probably why you get on so well with Julia, you both sense a lonely soul in the other."

A knock interrupted them before Hugh could respond to claim that they got on well because Julia was a termagant and had a sharp tongue, but the reality was that it was far more than something so simple. William had touched on a nerve, and Hugh wanted to deny it, refute that his life was anything but exactly how he liked it. Once again, though, he knew his words would no longer be convincing.

He was indeed a lonely soul. He could count only John as a real friend, everyone else he kept at arm's length. Even the mistresses he had taken over the years had been almost a business agreement. He wanted release, and they wanted money or other valuable items. It had seemed to suit them both, but it had been an empty existence.

Thinking the emptiness that he so often felt and the feelings of not actually belonging anywhere would have eased once he found Florence, he was disappointed and unsettled that they had not. There was nothing else he could think of which would remove it. Luckily, he had Julia's tormenting to keep him from becoming melancholy. He hoped she would be around for a long time to come, the house would seem empty without her.

"My lord, the doctor is here to check on you," Richards said for the second time after he had received no response from his first announcement.

"Show him to my chamber, I shall be there shortly," Hugh said, nodding to William and finishing his glass of wine. "Thank you for your company, it has been enlightening," he said to William before leaving the room.

William smiled when he was left alone. "Never been in love," he whispered to himself. "Deluded man, but he will learn the reality of his situation very soon."

Chapter 12

Julia took Florence to the next Bluestocking Club meeting. She had discussed it with Grace and they had agreed that a few small gatherings would be perfect to build up Florence's confidence, so that by the time she had her come out, there would be a few friendly faces in the ballrooms she attended.

Florence had been terrified. "What if I say something stupid?" she fussed as they travelled in the carriage to Grace's house where the meetings were always held.

"Everyone has said or done something foolish at some point, you will not receive condemnation from anyone if you do," Julia answered.

"But you are all friends and have known each other forever."

"Which is why I know you have no need to be in any doubt that you will be welcomed unreservedly."

"You have more faith in me than I have in myself," Florence moaned.

"That is because you cannot see what I can. Do not be quick to put yourself down; you are pretty, wealthy and come from one of the best families in London, that is enough to gain you access to every parlour around."

"Maybe so, but then I open my mouth and, *bang*, I am shown the servants' quarters."

Julia laughed. "You worry too much. I am taking you out to enjoy yourself, not to cause you a fit of the hysterics."

"I am as likely to do that as you are." There was more fire in Florence's words than in her previous utterances.

"Precisely, so stop worrying and enjoy the afternoon," Julia said.

Everyone greeted the newcomer with interest and pleasure but did not overwhelm her. There was a talk arranged by a woman who had done a Grand Tour across Europe with only her maid as companion, and they were all crying with laughter by the end of it.

"And that, ladies, is why you should never leave home without two pairs of stockings," the speaker said, and the room erupted with applause.

Julia leaned over to Florence. "Serena will be the first one to approach her, just watch." They smiled at each other as the blonde-haired woman was first out of her seat and across the room, immediately introducing herself. "She is desperate to have the same sort of adventures."

"I would be terrified," Florence said.

"Me too. I am definitely a home bird," Julia said. "Come, we can live vicariously through Serena and Miss Elliot, let us go and listen to them."

They approached the two women who were animatedly chatting and stood listening and laughing. Julia joined in the conversation occasionally, but Florence remained silent.

"I am having a party at my house before I set off for a trip across Africa," Miss Elliot said. "Everyone is invited." She smiled at Florence.

"Oh, but I could not," Florence said quickly.

"It is perfectly acceptable that you go to a house party of a friend," Julia said. "As long as you are with us, it will be fine."

"I cannot offer pirates and vagabonds," Miss Elliot said. "Although there may be raucous behaviour by some of the guests."

"I have had enough of vagabonds to last a lifetime," Florence said, surprising Julia that she would admit to something of her past.

"You are quite correct, vagabonds are tedious, but pirates, now they can be quite exquisite if you meet the right one."

Julia laughed. "Unfortunately, not many are found in the ballrooms of London."

"More's the pity for it would certainly liven things up," Miss Elliot said. "Now promise you will come to my party."

When Florence agreed, Miss Elliot excused herself and went to speak to the others, probably to offer the same invitation.

"I like her," Florence said.

"Me too," Julia said. "She obviously liked you, not everyone would extend the invitation to a girl barely out of the school room."

"Little does anyone know that I have never been in a school room," Florence said.

"But your mother did teach you useful lessons."

"Which I did not appreciate at the time. Now I would do anything to go back to those lessons and the time she insisted we spent together working, just to show her how much I appreciated her," Florence confessed.

"She knew," Julia said.

"I hope so."

"Right, now we have filled your head with all sorts tonight, let us return to your uncle's."

"Why are there not more women at your club?" Florence asked. There were more than the seven founder members in the audience, but it was made up of people who would appreciate something other than wishing to spend their evenings in one insipid drawing room or another.

"We are seen as the oddities of society," Julia said without sounding upset. "Not many women would want to be associated with a group of people who seem so unappealing.

"Why are you seen as so different to everyone else?"

"Because we do not rely on men for our education or information. We have curious minds that we do not deaden with mindless employment," Julia said.

"If that is the case," Florence said, hands on hips. "Why are you insisting that I learn that blasted embroidery?"

Julia laughed. "You are not to be like us, your destiny is to lie on a different path, on which you cannot use such base language." She thought it prudent not to mention she had used worse towards Hugh.

"A more tedious one by the sounds of it."

"Not at all," Grace interrupted the conversation. "You have not experienced the delights society has to offer. Have a few seasons and then decide whether it is the bluestocking life for you, none of us decided this was to be our path from the first instance. We all enjoyed a few seasons of frivolity before we discovered we did not wish it for the rest of our lives."

"You had seasons as I am expected to have?"

"Yes, only Julia here joined us during her first season. The rest of us had enjoyed two or three seasons."

"To be fair, I had delayed my come out," Julia said.

"Yes, you persuaded William to yet again do your bidding," Grace said with a knowing look.

Julia shrugged. "It suited us both at the time."

"Fine, I shall have a season and then officially become a member of your club," Florence said.

"We will talk about this once your first season is over," Grace said. "No promises until then. Ah, it looks like Miss Elliot is ready to leave."

Florence looked crestfallen at Grace's retreating back. "She doesn't want me to join, does she?"

"She does not wish a beautiful young lady to embrace the life of a spinster before she has experienced anything of the world," Julia explained. "Try everything and then make an informed decision, it is good advice not to rush into anything."

"I will have to run away with a pirate if I am to escape society then," Florence said, sounding like the young girl she was.

"As you wish, but please wait until my being your chaperone is at an end. I cannot imagine what your uncle would say if I managed to lose you after all his time searching for you."

"Oh, damn it, I forgot about how kind Uncle Hugh is being, I could not hurt him."

"Florence, you really do need to curb your tongue."

"But I am from the streets of London, ah'll 'ave you know," Florence responded, falling into the accent of the streets.

"Who will be the death of me," Julia groaned with a grin.

***

Florence was excited by the time the party came around. She had been to another gathering with Julia's friends and they were all treating her as something between a younger sister or daughter, and she was blossoming under their attentions.

She knocked on Julia's chamber door as soon as she was dressed and entered at Julia's acknowledgement.

"Oh, you look beautiful," Florence said as she looked at Julia's plain lilac silk gown with an embroidered overskirt. "Those flowers must have taken weeks."

"Now you appreciate the women who can embroider," Julia said.

"Just be thankful you do not have to rely on me for your adornments, or you would have to wait years for every new dress," Florence said. "Will I do?"

"You look very well indeed," Julia said. "You are lucky to suit a white muslin gown, many debutantes look sickly without colour to enhance their complexion, but your more olive skin suits it perfectly."

Florence beamed at the compliment. "Uncle Hugh says if all goes to plan, he will be happy for me to have my come out next year, which is really daunting. I hoped it would be further away. He insisted that I need more polish, and I pointed out that he had better delay my first season for ten years if he is waiting for me to be perfect."

"Nonsense, you could pass as any other debutante," Julia chided. "You are just a little young, so his lordship is quite correct to delay until next year. I am sure if you still do not feel ready, he would delay it further."

"I hope so. Oh, he said to mention that he is dropping us off at the party, he said it's on the way to his club and he will collect us later."

"Come, let us not keep him waiting," Julia said, fastening the pearl bracelet around her wrist and glancing one last time in the mirror.

As they walked down the stairs, Hugh was waiting at the bottom. "My, my, I am glad this will be a gathering for women alone, or you would both be receiving offers by the end of the evening. You look stunning."

Julia flashed Florence a look. "I did not lead him to believe that it was a female-only gathering, did you?"

"No," Florence said, but she flushed.

"Florence!" Hugh said. "Who is going to be at this party?" he demanded.

"Vagabonds and pirates, hopefully, but she only actually promised vagabonds," Florence answered in mock innocence.

"Good God, you have promised her what?" Hugh turned to Julia.

"Now just wait one moment before you run away with yourself! It would not be good for someone your age to have apoplexy in the hall. I promised Florence nothing of the sort, Miss Elliot was teasing her. It will be a respectable gathering, or I would not be attending," Julia said, her expression revealing exactly what she thought about his accusations.

"Then I apologise." Hugh bowed his head. "I need to speak to my niece about how she delivers information and about telling stories that might get others into trouble."

"That's cursing, jesting, and goodness knows what else I can't do," Florence grumbled. "I might as well not say a word."

"Exactly. Now come on, brat. I have the urge for a large glass of whiskey, and I have to drop you off first in order to reach it," Hugh said, ushering them out of the door when they had put on their cloaks with the help of the ever-efficient footmen.

"Just think yourself lucky that you do not have to watch her all evening. I would employ a companion with a strong constitution if I were you," Julia said.

"I can hear you both!" Florence shouted from inside the carriage.

"Lord above, she sounds like a fishwife," Hugh moaned, but winked at Julia's laugh.

Chapter 13

Hugh handed Florence an invitation three days later. “You must have made a good impression, brat. You have been invited to a small, private party held by Benedict Wilkinson.”

“Oh, he spoke to me quite a lot at Miss Elliot’s party,” Florence said with pleasure. “He was very nice.”

“He is too old for you,” Hugh said quickly.

Julia did not try to hide her eye roll. “She is allowed to like men without forming an attachment to them,” she said.

“I was just being clear about my opinion,” Hugh defended himself.

Julia shook her head. “You will see at Mr Wilkinson’s party that he looks on her as a mere child.”

“Which she is.”

“Which I am not.”

“I am almost sorry that I am not to be your constant companion, Florence. I can only imagine what sparks will fly when you are presented at court,” Julia said.

"I need to find a companion at the earliest opportunity, if only to stop your gloating at the trials and tribulations Florence is going to cause me," Hugh said, smiling when she glared at him.

"Have you placed an advert yet?" Julia asked.

Hugh looked discomfited. "No, not so far. I was trying to think of any suitable relatives I might have in the first instance." The reality was, he was trying to delay any appointment as long as possible so that he did not have to say goodbye to Julia. He had spent more time at home these last weeks than he had ever done, and it had only been a little to do with Florence. Drawn to Julia like he had never been to anyone else before, he knew he was being selfish in wanting to prolong her visit for as long as he could.

"How many relatives do you have?" Julia asked.

"I am not sure. Not many, I suppose," Hugh admitted.

"And it has taken you weeks to discover them?"

"It is not an easy task finding the right person," Hugh muttered.

"Is my reputation so poor within the family that no one will come?" Florence looked mortified.

"Not at all!" Hugh quickly reassured her. "It is I putting off the job, that is all. I cannot remember ever liking any of my relatives, therefore I am trying to decide who will bore me the least. It has nothing to do with you, I assure you. I will send letters out tomorrow."

"As long as you are sure," Florence said. "Although the longer it takes, the more time we spend with Julia, and I cannot be upset about that."

Hugh blushed, and his colour deepened at the surprised expression Julia shot in his direction. "I shall go and attend to it now," he said gruffly, leaving the room.

"That touched a nerve," Florence said with a grin. "How long has Uncle Hugh been sweet on you?"

"He is not." Julia was now the one to flush. She wished she did not have to try to brush off the reaction Hugh had to Florence's words. Was he delaying sending for someone because he liked her?

She must admit, she was in no hurry to return to Half Moon Street, and Uncle William had never mentioned anything about wanting to return, but she had not thought Hugh felt the same way. Especially as there had been no other hints since the words he had uttered when he was injured. Could he hold her in affection? Or was it just her interpreting his delay wrongly, and it was nothing more than a man taking the easiest route to solve a problem?

Noticing Florence's smiling face, she frowned at her, but her tone was not serious. "Any more of your impudence and I shall remove myself and Uncle William at our earliest convenience."

Florence laughed. “I am so tempted to test that theory, because I have a sneaking suspicion that you and Uncle Hugh are of the same mind.”

“Tsk.”

“I will be delighted, by the way, if there is an announcement.”

“I do believe I will be visiting Serena alone today,” Julia said, standing and loftily brushing herself down.

“Aww please, don’t leave me here to practice my needlework,” Florence wailed.

“I have a good mind to, just to put you in your place.”

“I promise not to mention anything else about my uncle being smitten with you,” Florence said, batting her eyes in such an outrageous way that Julia could not help but laugh.

“You are a minx.”

“I know, but you like me, despite that.”

“You remind me too much of myself.”

“Oh, that’s praise indeed!”

“Is it? I suddenly have the desire to write to my old governess and apologise profusely.”

***

Hugh avoided Julia and Florence as much as he could for the next few days, not easy when living under the same roof. He silently cursed his niece to the devil for the smug look she shot him every time he entered a room and Julia was there.

Thankfully, Julia was the same as always with him, infuriating and challenging, but that was when he loved her company the most. She made him laugh so often with her retorts that he went to bed every night, his stomach muscles aching. To see him laugh at all would have astounded most members of the *ton*, but to see him constantly in fits of mirth would have probably sent them into complete shock. He was struggling with the realisation that he enjoyed the lighter side of life, being teased and teasing in return. He could not remember when life had become so serious, but it had altered since Julia had come into it and he was thankful of the change.

Since finding Florence, he felt lighter, more at peace, having been able to right some of the wrong his parents had caused, but a lot of his contentment was due to Julia staying with them. Having been forced to send a letter asking a distant cousin if she was willing to be Florence's companion, he now chose to ignore the fact that one day Julia would leave and although they would remain friends, it would never be the same as her being under the same roof as him.

At the Wilkinson's gathering he had watched Julia with other guests and could not believe that he had never noticed her before. She seemed so vivacious and soon had the gentlemen laughing who were lucky enough to be seated next to her throughout dinner.

Mr Wilkinson had invited other guests to join them after the meal and led the diners into the ballroom to mix with the newcomers. Hugh had danced with Florence first, but his second was with Julia.

"We are being watched, my lord," she said as they crossed in the set.

Hugh scowled. "Why she is here, goodness only knows," he said of Kathryn, who had arrived with her latest conquest. That she had spent the last hour glowering at Hugh had not gone unnoticed.

"She is clearly a prize men want to show off," Julia said.

"You really should not be aware of what she is, let alone discussing it with me," Hugh pointed out.

"My not mentioning it would not change the situation."

"No, but..."

"But it would make you less discomfited?"

"Probably."

"Yet, I am supposing that at some point you acted in the same way with her as Mr Patrick is doing now."

"I do not see your point." Hugh did not want to acknowledge that he had shared anything with Kathryn, she had definitely been a mistake on his part, but he especially did not want to discuss it with Julia.

Hating the fact that she must think ill of him, he scowled at her.

Julia laughed. "It is just that you cannot criticise someone for doing what you did. I actually feel sorry for her, even though she is sending daggers at us."

"Why in God's name would you feel sorry for her? As you seem to know so much about the situation, I feel compelled to inform you that your sentiments are wasted. You do realise that she would laugh to realise you pitied her, don't you?" Hugh asked incredulously.

"Oh, I am perfectly aware what she thinks of the likes of me," Julia said. "But at some point in the future, there will be no one knocking on her door to escort her around town. She will only be welcomed into society for as long as her looks last, which at the current state of her looks is not too far from now."

Hugh startled the dancers around him by his crack of laughter at Julia's words. "I have never met anyone like you, Miss Marsh. You have just offered sympathy whilst insulting her at the same time. That is a skill indeed."

"I never said I was perfect." Julia grinned at him. "But I am speaking the truth, and I do feel sorry for her, at least to some extent."

"You are an utter delight," Hugh said, smiling one of his rare, genuine smiles.

"Thank you," Julia said, for once accepting the compliment.

***

The three entered Bryn House in the early hours of the morning, tired but having enjoyed a lively evening. Florence was gaining in confidence, and it was clear that the people she met liked her.

They were disrobing shawls, gloves and hats in the hallway when an almighty crash sounded from the morning room at the front of the house.

"Stay there!" Hugh commanded as Richards, himself and a footman ran into the room.

Julia had moved to Florence and linked her arm as they waited. It was only seconds before the footman burst back out of the room and, flinging open the front door, ran out into the street. They heard his footsteps thunder across the pavement.

Hearing a noise from upstairs, Julia was relieved to see it was Uncle William, worriedly looking over the banister rail. "Julia, what on earth is going on?"

"I am not quite sure, Uncle," Julia answered. "But we are all well."

Hugh returned from the morning room, holding a brick in his hand and glaring at a piece of paper. Before he could speak, the footman returned, breathless but shaking his head.

"You saw nothing?" Hugh demanded.

"A figure running, but he had such a head start on me, I could not catch him, my lord. I am sorry."

"Whoever did this will be sorry," Hugh growled out. "Richards, the window needs securing."

"I shall make sure it's safe, m'lud, and have someone positioned there all night to be doubly sure," Richards said, giving a silent instruction to the footman who was still gasping for breath, but who nodded in understanding.

"What does the note say?" Julia asked.

"You owe me," Hugh answered.

"Have you any debts we should be aware of?" Julia asked, trying to lighten the mood.

Hugh smiled at her, appreciating that she did not seem affected in any way by the incident. He knew of many who would be swooning at what had happened. "None that would resort to a broken window. I cannot think who would... Surely she would not..."

Julia understood who he was referring to, although the others might not. She did not wish to be a part of the conversation if it was to involve that blasted woman. For some reason, a jealous previous mistress had been diverting in the ballroom, but late at night, attacking the house, it was suddenly not so amusing.

"Come, Florence, there is nothing we can do here, let us go to bed." It was only as she looked at Florence that Julia saw how pale she was. "Florence, what is it? We are safe, I assure you. Your uncle and the staff are more than capable of providing a guard over us."

"Th-the note," Florence stammered.

"It probably means nothing," Julia soothed.

"It is what *he* said."

"What who said?" Hugh demanded, approaching Florence.

"Jack. On the night you found me, when he knew the fight was lost, he said that I owed him. This must be him; who else could it be? He's found me!"

Hugh and Julia exchanged a look. "I think we should go to the drawing room and send for some hot chocolate, and you can explain everything to us," Julia said gently. "Or you can just tell your uncle, whichever you wish, but he needs to know all about this Jack, whoever he is."

Florence gripped Julia's arm. "Please stay."

"Of course I will."

Hugh gave the order for drinks to be served and the three moved into the drawing room. Julia had assured Uncle William there was no need for him to remain out of bed, and he had nodded his night-capped head in understanding and withdrawn to his bedchamber.

The three sat on one sofa, Hugh next to Florence, Julia on her other side. "What does this man think you owe him?" Hugh asked gently. "Please tell me everything. All I want to do is to protect you, and the best way of doing that is to know what we are facing."

"Thank you," Florence said. "But you might feel different after I tell you it all, and I will understand, I promise. I knew this was too good to last."

Chapter 14

"Tell me," Hugh said gently.

Florence sighed, shoulders drooping. "Ma never sold herself to raise money, no matter how hungry or cold we were."

Julia saw Hugh stiffen and wished she could offer him support. Holding one of Florence's hands, she reached behind Florence's back and squeezed Hugh's upper arm, it was the only thing she could do. He looked at her, but she could see from his expression of gratitude that she had done the right thing.

"You have mentioned that before," Julia said. "She sounds like she was a very principled lady."

"She used to get teased by the people we knew. They would call her princess because she had airs and graces which didn't fit into the lives we were leading, but she refused to let go of her upbringing. She would always say it did not matter where she was in the world, she would always be the daughter of an earl, and that came with the responsibility to be respectable and decent."

Hugh looked anguished. "I will never stop cursing my father and mother for the damage they did to you both."

"Ma used to say it was her own fault. She cursed her parents too, but at the end of the day she always admitted that she was the one who had been foolish," Florence said.

"Probably just seeking love anywhere she could find it, for there was none in any of our houses," Hugh said bitterly.

Julia ached for him, but waited to hear the rest of the story with dread.

"She never forgot about you," Florence said. "She would talk about how mischievous you were as a little boy."

"Until it was beaten out of me," Hugh said.

"She said how you would insist that only she could read your stories in the way you liked them, and I completely understand why. She did the same with me, but from memory for we had no books."

Hugh smiled sadly. "She would make up the most outrageous voices for the characters and would never get mixed up, getting louder and louder as the story came to its conclusion."

"And then tickling you and telling you that the monsters would come if she heard a sound from you before..."

"Whispering that she would always be there to fight off any monsters," Hugh said, his voice cracking.

Tears started pouring down Florence's face and Julia wrapped an arm around her. "She used to promise me that, and she did until she died," Florence said.

They were interrupted by the arrival of the tea tray with three cups of hot chocolate. Richards did not say a word, but put the tray down and left the room, closing the door behind him.

Julia gave Florence a cup, wrapping her fingers around the warmth, before she did the same with Hugh. He looked in surprise at the contact as her fingers covered his. "Drink, it will help," Julia said before picking up her own cup and seating herself next to Florence once more.

They drank in silence for a few moments; it was clear both Hugh and Florence were deep in thought about the past. Eventually, Hugh put his empty cup on the table and turned to Florence. "How was she able to protect you? Was your father around?"

Julia was surprised to realise that Florence had confided in her more than she had her uncle, but then it was sometimes easier to talk to a stranger, and Hugh had been injured when she had first come into their lives.

"I never knew him," Florence answered. "When he realised he wasn't going to get hold of any of mother's inheritance, he left."

"How did you both survive?"

"Mother would do any job going, cleaning, mending, washing, anything as long as it did not involve selling her body," Florence said proudly. "There was a man, Mark. I think he liked Ma, but nothing ever happened between them. He was a good friend to have, though. He looked out for us in a way that shielded us from the worst of what we could have faced, I am sure of it. He was well respected in the neighbourhood, and anyone who was under his protection was left alone."

"Was he a criminal?" Hugh asked.

"I do not know. Honestly. And I do not care, he never did us any harm." She paused. "I suppose he could have been for his death was brutal."

"I do not suppose it matters," Hugh said.

"Ma died last year," Florence said, tears in her eyes once more. "I have never felt so alone, but Mark visited me and gave me some money. He promised that while he was around, I was safe, but he did say that I would be better trying to get into service or something. I wondered after he died if he knew someone was after him." Florence shrugged. "I couldn't go into service, though. I helped Ma whenever I could, but I had no experience or references, so I tried to get jobs like Ma had done to make Mark's money last as long as possible."

"Where is she buried?" Hugh suddenly asked.

"In a pauper's grave," Florence said sadly.

Hugh leaned forward, rubbing his hands over his face. "I will do something in the family crypt for her."

"Thank you. I know she won't be there, but it would be nice to be able to visit a gravestone," Florence said. "It would be as if she has not completely gone, which it felt like after she died."

"When did Mark die?" Julia asked.

"Six months ago," Florence said. "Everyone was shocked, but like I said, I don't know if he suspected that someone was trying to take over his businesses. After Mark died, Jack stopped me in the street one day. He offered... he offered me protection if I would be his girl."

Hugh had paled, hands fisted and jaw tense.

"But you refused," Julia said, to quickly ease the sudden tension in the room.

"I did, but he kept on and on. Everywhere I went, he would appear, he even sent me flowers a few times. I was still in the room that I had rented with Ma, Mark's money and the little I was earning meant that I could keep a roof over my head, but I decided that I couldn't stay there any longer, so I moved."

"It must have been terrifying for you, being without support against a determined man," Julia sympathised.

"It was because it really felt that no one cared. Jack was feared, so I would get no support from anyone, the only thing I could think of was to move away, so I did. I had two weeks' peace and then he found me again."

Hugh jumped up from his seat. "I should have been out every single night looking for you instead of pretending I was searching while wasting my time in some stupid ballroom or other."

"Oh no! It isn't your fault, it's no one's fault." Florence stood and went to Hugh.

He embraced her, and Julia felt a prickling of tears behind her eyes. She was certain that this was a turning point in their relationship, and she was so happy for them both; even though there was pain to go through, eventually they would find so much comfort in each other. They deserved it, both of them had been lost for so long.

Hugh eventually held Florence at arm's length. "I promise you this, I will never leave you unprotected again. Even when I am old and grey, there will be something in place which will ensure that you are safe. Wherever you are and whatever you are doing, you will never be so vulnerable again."

"Thank you," Florence whispered, tears pouring once more. She hiccupped a laugh. "I have never cried so much in my life as I have tonight."

"That is because you know you are home and are safe," Hugh said, embracing her once more.

"I still have nightmares about how close I came to ruination," Florence said.

"What happened? When I got to you, you were surrounded by those men," Hugh said.

"Yes, Jack had tracked me down and was putting the pressure on again. But I think he was losing patience because he was becoming more threatening and sending his men to intimidate me, and it was working. I had given up hope of any escape from him, and in a weak moment, I agreed that I would be his girl."

Hugh's sharp intake of breath was masked by Florence's fresh burst of tears, but Julia saw how her words had shocked and angered him on her behalf.

"But I couldn't," Florence sobbed. "I just kept thinking how Ma had avoided selling herself and yet here I was about to do the one thing that she would have hated me to do. Jack had promised to pay for everything I needed, that my worries would be over, but it made me ill to think of what I would have to do to get that peace of mind. I would be swapping one nightmare for another. I decided I just could not face that future and left my new room. I was trying to earn money but not to live anywhere, and it wasn't working..."

Julia pressed a clean handkerchief into Florence's hand as she took a deep breath and continued, "I could barely sleep, always afraid that I was going to be robbed or worse, so I spent most of the night wandering around the streets, which were scary despite being afraid that Jack would find me. He did, of course, but then you appeared. I did not know who you were then, but I was never so thankful to see a gentleman in my life, especially when you started to confront Jack and tell him I was your family. I was terrified for you and hoping you wouldn't leave all at the same time."

"He came with support, he was clearly determined to make sure you were under his control," Hugh said, teeth still gritted.

"I don't know what he intended, but I am so glad you were there, both of you," she said, smiling at Julia. "But now it looks like he has found me again."

"We do not know that for sure," Julia said.

"It is his style," Florence said. "He is not subtle."

"Neither am I," Hugh said. "There will be more footmen employed tomorrow and more accompanying you to and from wherever you go. You will not be left alone, and he will eventually give up."

"I do not think he will, I have been here for weeks and it looks like he has been looking for me. I had hoped he would lose interest, but it seems he is very determined, which means at some point I will be ruined."

"What he does not know is that I am a stubborn brute, and you are under my protection now and always will be," Hugh said. "I will also be visiting Bow Street and reporting that he was the one who stabbed me and issuing a reward for his capture. That should help to keep him focused on keeping away from you. If you have his surname?"

"Jack Anderson," Florence said.

"I think enough has been gone over for tonight," Julia said. "Time for bed, otherwise the sun will be rising before we get any sleep. Florence, I do not mind spending the night in your chamber if you would feel more comfortable."

"Oh, would you? Thank you. I know it is foolish, but I think I would sleep better if you were with me."

"It is not foolish in the slightest, I will also rest easier knowing you are not alone," Julia said. "Good night, my lord."

"Thank you," Hugh said. "There will be someone outside your room all night."

"Do you think that is necessary?" Julia asked.

"I just want to be sure." Hugh smiled slightly.

"Ah, so you will sleep easier," Julia said with a grin.

"You have guessed my motivation. Selfish as always," Hugh responded, ruffling Florence's hair. "Sleep well, brat. You are not alone."

Chapter 15

Julia was first down to the dining room in the morning. She felt that she had heard every noise in the night, and when Hugh walked in, she smiled at him. "You look how I feel. A disturbed night, my lord?"

"Yes. It was a relief when morning finally came. To say we retired so late, it felt like the longest time before I could rise," Hugh said, pouring himself a coffee and drinking it before pouring another.

"I did not raise it last night because Florence was so sure of who the offender was, but you suspected someone else first," Julia said.

"I have thought about that," Hugh said. "It is not in her style. She would more likely find a more subtle way of hurting me."

"She would be brave to do that."

"One who is feeling wronged often is not thinking straight. That she had already started to see Patrick before I ended what we had shared has been conveniently forgotten."

"What a life! I hope you choose someone more sensible for your next conquest."

Hugh stared at her for a moment before chuckling. "I cannot believe I am having this conversation with you over the breakfast table, but I do not think anything should surprise me where you are concerned, Miss Marsh. I can honestly say that how sensible a woman is, is not usually a consideration when choosing a mistress."

Julia pursed her lips, trying to hide the real feeling of displeasure she felt at his words.

"What have I said to receive that silent curse?" Hugh asked.

"There is nothing wrong with being sensible," Julia huffed.

Laughing, Hugh shook his head at her. "Do not bamboozle me by trying to convince me that you consider yourself sensible, or I shall declare you the ninnyhammer you must be."

"Well, of all the..."

"Before you snap my nose off," Hugh said. "Let me remind you that you were the one racing through London trying to save the fools who put themselves at risk. If Florence had declared she was doing that, pray what would your reaction be?"

"She is a lot younger than I," Julia said defensively.

"And has spent a lot more time on the streets. You are many things, Miss Marsh, but sensible is not one of them."

"You are trying to bring me around by pretending that is a compliment, but it is so clearly an insult."

"Take it as you wish."

"You really are a nodcock of the worst kind!" Julia said in annoyance.

"I have been considered far worse."

"I am not surprised."

Florence entered the room at Hugh's laugh and looked between the two of them, saying nothing. Filling her plate from the side table, she glanced at Julia over her shoulder. "I must say that I am glad of our talk today at the Bluestocking Club. I think it might come in useful."

"What talk is it this time?" Hugh asked with a glint in his eye aimed in Julia's direction. "Is it needlework, or discussing the latest novel?"

"Mr Angelo is coming along to discuss the art of fencing and to show us how we can use everyday items such as our parasols to defend ourselves, should we need to," Julia replied smugly.

Both women noticed the arrested expression on Hugh's face, as if he had been struck forcibly by something, but neither could guess what it could be.

Eventually, Julia broke the silence. "Are you considering how dangerous it will become when passing the stand containing our canes and parasols, my lord?"

"No. I am wondering something else entirely," Hugh answered, but he gave no further indication of what had struck him.

They were interrupted by Richards, who announced that Mr Carmichael had called.

Hugh stood. "I asked John to call on me and hope to enlist his help over the coming weeks, until Jack Anderson is put away," he said.

"Oh, please do not!" Florence said. "I will not be able to face him if he knows how foolish I have been."

"He only needs to know the basic details," Hugh assured her. "It would be useful to have another who can access the parties we can. I want as many around you as possible for both our peace of minds."

Florence nodded in resignation as Hugh left the room.

He did not go immediately to the morning room to see John, instead he went to his study and stood before the window. Looking out over the garden at the back of his home, he leaned against the wooden surround. Julia had stunned him. Time and again she surprised him, but something else had happened when she had spoken of Angelo coming to speak to the ladies of her group. He had realised something that had probably happened weeks ago, but he had refused to acknowledge it. He was in love. Completely and utterly in love with a woman who had turned his world upside down, yet was providing something he had never felt before. Love. She was everything, funny, intelligent, compassionate, and he needed her in his life forever.

Wishing he could seek her out and ask her immediately for her hand, he paused, there were two reasons he could not. He was certain she liked him, but he had the sneaking suspicion she thought he was some sort of arrogant fool, which he was quite often, or had been before he had met her. He wanted to be sure that she would receive his approach with pleasure and not laugh in his face. Someone who had never been in love before and had seen how destructive love could be to a family needed to be certain before he committed his heart and his life to someone.

The second reason for his hesitation was Florence. He needed to make sure she was safe before he started to plan a wedding. A week or two delay would not matter in the long term, he thought with a smile. Miss Marsh would be worth the wait.

Content that he had everything under control, he went to join his friend.

***

Florence had come back from the Bluestocking Club in high spirits and had insisted that she be allowed to practice with Hugh and John, who had spent the afternoon organising Hugh's household and assessing which entertainments they could attend.

John had laughed and been the first to volunteer to be the target, and he and Florence sparred whilst Hugh watched, criticising his friend for weak responses and poor step work.

"Your uncle is a bore where fencing or boxing is involved," John finally admitted when he had experienced enough stomach pokes with a cane for one day.

"Will you give me boxing lessons, Uncle?" Florence asked.

"I most certainly will not," Hugh answered. "I do not want both the ladies under my roof visiting Gentleman Jackson." The moment the words were out of his mouth, he realised he had made a huge error.

John and Florence were staring open-mouthed at him.

"Forget I said that, I was teasing."

"You are not in your dotage just yet," John said. "Miss Marsh is the young woman Jackson has been training all this time?"

"Blast it! If she finds out I have revealed her secret, she will draw my cork."

"Why would she need to have lessons?" John asked, clearly not about to let the matter drop.

Hugh shrugged. "She has an interest in pugilism."

John sat down, crossing his legs. "This is coming it too brown, what are you hiding from us?"

Florence had been stock still, frowning at something she was trying to recall. "She never told me why she was in the area that we were in on the night you found me," she said. "With all the excitement about being here and everything I have had to learn, it slipped my mind, but I remember now. She was dressed in—"

"Florence, enough!" Hugh interrupted. "It is not for us to speculate about Miss Marsh."

"I can hardly believe I am saying this, but she is the shadow," Florence said, not taking the hint that her uncle wanted to stop her revealing who Julia was.

John laughed. "Miss Marsh? No! She is too fine to be running through the streets at night, fighting. Hugh? What is wrong? Good Lord! I can see by your expression, it is true, is it not? Well, I never! What an absolute lark!"

"It is no lark," Hugh said through gritted teeth. "She is no longer involved in that side of life."

"The news reports say differently," John pointed out.

"They are either making stories up or there are people who are imitating her," Hugh said.

"Well, well, well. Are you sure you need my help? All you need is Miss Marsh, and Miss Weston will be perfectly safe."

"Do not be a fool," Hugh snapped. "Of course I need your help."

John sobered, knowing he had gone too far with his teasing. "I was funning, that is all. I will not breathe a word of this discovery and of course I will help. I am and always will be at your service, Hugh."

"Thank you."

John soon took his leave; the change in atmosphere between uncle and niece had made it so that he was sure they needed to speak without his presence.

Florence had remained silent after her first outburst, and only when John left did she speak. "She has not been honest with me, when I have told her everything," she said quietly.

"It is not as simple as that," Hugh defended Julia.

"Is it not?"

"No. She could be ruined if it was revealed what she was doing."

"I am not exactly in a position to criticise anyone for not being perfect in the eyes of society, but I considered that we were friends."

"You are."

"So much so that she has kept a whole chunk of her life a secret from me."

"You said she mentioned that she would tell you about it one day, perhaps she has not felt comfortable telling you. It is a big secret to reveal."

"And so was the story about Jack, but I wanted her there. I feel like I do not know her," Florence said.

Julia unfortunately entered the room at that moment and noticed the glare she received from Florence. "Is there anything amiss?"

"I know your secret," Florence snapped.

"Oh."

"It was my fault," Hugh confessed. "I let slip about your lessons at the club."

"You were not honest with me," Florence said.

"I am sorry I have not told you, but it never seemed the appropriate time, and I know how much Uncle William lives in fear of it being discovered, so I was doubly hesitant to mention anything."

"I was clearly not trustworthy enough to know."

"That is not true."

"Of course it is. I have told you everything there is to know about me, no matter how bad it was. I did that because I thought we were friends, I now realise any connection we shared was one-sided."

Julia crossed the room to Florence and held out her hands to her, but they dropped to her side when Florence did not put her hands in hers. "I promise you it had nothing to do with you, or what I feel about you that kept me from telling you."

"Those are easy words to say."

"They are, but they are meant most sincerely. You are fully aware of how society can turn against a person who does not conform. Luckily, you have the backing of an earl, who has friends of equal or higher ranking. I have my uncle, who I love dearly and would not change for the world, but could you imagine the speculation and ridicule we would receive if it was revealed who I was? The mad inventor and his niece who dresses as a man and roams the streets at night? Who would take either of us seriously if that was common knowledge?"

"I suppose it would have caused a stir," Florence admitted reluctantly.

"You liked my uncle from the moment you met him. I love him for being the man who took me in when he was a bachelor, with no experience of dealing with a young child in mourning, but he did it without hesitation and has never made me feel like the slightest burden to him. I could never repay his kindness or his love by being the cause of society turning their back on him."

"He is very kind and welcomed me immediately."

"He even improved my fortune, bless him. He could have taken most of the money and invested into his inventions, I offered it enough times, but he would not. He was determined that I would have an independence, for he is comfortable but has not unlimited funds. Again and again, he has been understanding beyond what was required of him, and although I could not stop the drive I had to protect others, I did it with every effort not to put my uncle at risk," Julia said, tears in her eyes.

"I just wish you had told me," Florence said, the anger no longer in her voice at the impassioned words from Julia.

"I am sorry that I did not," Julia said. "But you are not alone, it was a secret I told to no one."

"Not even your friends?" Florence asked.

"Grace knows since she visited when I still sported a bruise and had been involved with your rescue. She guessed most of it, having had suspicions before then, but none of the others know anything."

Florence looked slightly mollified at Julia's answer.

"John knows," Hugh said.

"Good grief! Should I take an advert out in the newspaper and make an announcement?" Julia said, exasperated.

"He will not mention it."

"You had better be right," Julia huffed. "I am sorry, Florence. I cannot apologise enough for remaining silent on the subject. I should have told you, but it is quite scary to have a secret which can ruin you and the person you love."

"I do understand. After all, my own background could do the same if that became public knowledge,"

Florence said. “It was a shock to hear, and I just felt the fool, as if I did not know you at all.”

“You do know me, and I would hate this to affect our friendship. I consider you as close a friend as any one of the club’s members. Speaking of which, they are going to be attending Mrs Tindall’s gathering tomorrow,” Julia said.

“That is good to know. I promised to compare notes with Serena on how much we have been practising when I next see her,” Florence said, no longer angry with Julia.

“I think we had better prepare ourselves for some violent encounters if we step out of line in the future, if all of you insist on practising,” Hugh said, trying to change the subject.

“Most certainly. Especially if gentlemen cannot hold their tongues,” Julia responded ominously.

Chapter 16

"How are you faring in the role of chaperone?" Grace asked Julia as they stood at the edge of the room in which Mrs Tindall had arranged an impromptu dance.

"Strange," Julia said. "One moment I feel old enough to be her mother, the next as if I have only just left the school room. It is very disconcerting."

Grace smiled. "I still feel like that sometimes, although my body is more likely to feel the creep of age these days."

"Nonsense! You were partaking fully of the fencing lesson Mr Angelo was giving us."

"I was, and for the next day I could hardly move. I hope you do not mind my saying something which I have observed recently; I have noticed that you are being glared at these last few gatherings when there has been a certain lady present."

Julia sighed. "Lord Weston's discarded mistress has taken a dislike to me. I really do not understand why, his separating from her had nothing to do with me."

"But the change in him has everything to do with you," Grace said. "Anyone who knows him knew how taciturn and withdrawn he always was; now look at him."

As Julia spent most of her time looking at Hugh wherever they were, she turned immediately to where he was dancing with Florence. "He is happy now his niece is safe," she said.

"I do not believe for a moment that is the only reason for the change, it is too profound."

Julia flushed. "You are mistaken. We are just friends."

"If you say so."

Grace was correct about Kathryn glaring at Julia, but her frown turned into a smile when Hugh passed her by, Florence on his arm, once the dance had ended.

"My lord, how good it is to see you," she purred.

Hugh bowed his head in her direction, but he had not intended to remain with her. Unfortunately, Mr Patrick had already been primed by his new love and was still besotted enough to do her bidding.

"Weston, is this your niece? Fine young woman. Would you do me the honour of introducing us so I can have the next dance with such a delight?"

"Florence, this is Mr Patrick. Patrick, my niece," Hugh said ungraciously.

"Delighted, my dear. Please tell me there is no beau on the edges of the dance floor, waiting to snatch you up."

"Do not be ridiculous, Patrick!" Hugh said.

"Your uncle is as cold as ice," Mr Patrick mock-whispered to Florence.

Florence smiled. "I am not engaged for the next dance and would be pleased to accept your hand. Thank you."

"Capital! At least one of the family is a joy to be around, eh Kathryn? I understand why you got sick of him, my dear," he said, putting Florence's hand on his arm and leading her away.

Hugh almost growled at their retreating forms, wishing he could stop Florence having to suffer the next half-hour with such a buffoon.

"Do not worry, my lord. He is harmless enough," Kathryn whispered into his ear, getting far closer than she should.

"He would have me to deal with if he was not," Hugh ground out, taking a step away from her.

His move angered her, and she decided it was time to deliver the dig she had been wishing to for days. "There is speculation about that your delightful niece is going to be joining the Bluestockings fully," she started. "It would be such a pity to see one so pretty and with so much potential wasting herself with a bunch of spinsters who terrify most of the men in society."

"You are being ridiculous. Accompanying Miss Marsh on a few meetings is hardly becoming a life-long member," Hugh scoffed.

"But you know how rumours start and how perceptions are set so early in a girl's season. She is not out yet, but people are taking notice of her, and who would not? She is pretty and looks the perfect young lady." She failed to notice the twitch of his lips at her comment, as Hugh thought of the times when Florence fell back into her broad accent and cursed as well as any man at whatever task she was trying to complete and was frustrating her.

"Her fortune, her family and her personality will ensure she is accepted wherever she goes."

"I hope that is that case, but heed the words of someone who knows what it is to be like to always be on the edges of society; it can be a very lonely place," Kathryn said before moving away.

Hugh watched Florence, a frown creasing his brow. She was spending a lot of time with the Bluestockings, and Kathryn was right about one thing, society could turn cruel so easily and sometimes without needing much of an excuse. He would have a word with Julia about it later. She would know what to do for the best.

***

It was the following morning before Hugh and Julia were alone, and he raised the subject of Florence spending less time with Julia's friends and more time with other members of the *ton*.

Julia sat in silence, listening but never commenting as Hugh prattled on with his reasons for his request. She concentrated on cutting her ham and eggs into small pieces, an action which Hugh eventually noticed was out of the ordinary, and his speech stumbled to a close, unused to Julia being so unresponsive.

"I am sure you understand what my concerns are?" Hugh asked when it was clear he was not going to get a reaction to what he had said. For some reason her silence was unnerving him; it was disconcerting.

"No. I do not," Julia answered.

"Oh. I thought it was perfectly straightforward."

"It is, I suppose. You are saying that my friends were good enough for your niece when she was first venturing out into this harsh society of ours, but now she is gaining confidence, you would rather people like me be kept away from her."

"I am not saying that at all!" Hugh exclaimed. "I just think less time with confirmed spinsters might be a good idea."

Julia raised her hand. “Stop. Enough of this! What has really altered your perspective? Why this change? I would be grateful for the real reason you seem to suddenly find my company so unappealing.”

“You know full well that I enjoy your company immensely, I am not saying that you are unwelcome in any regard. I have relied on you so much these last weeks, it would be churlish at best and downright ungrateful for me to repay your help and support in such a way. But I have been led to believe that one or two people are starting to make comments about who Florence is associating with,” Hugh tried to explain, but he flushed when he saw Julia narrow her eyes.

“This is quite sudden, is it not? Almost as if something happened yesterday to alter your opinion. The only person you were in a tête-à-tête with last evening was that blasted woman, was it not?”

“I did not have a tête-à-tête! We exchanged a few words, nothing more. It would be unreasonable for me to completely ignore her, as much as I do not wish to associate with her anymore.”

“I have eyes, my lord, and I flatter myself that I have some modicum of intelligence,” Julia snapped. “Was it about my group of friends and myself that she was whispering to you?”

At any other moment Hugh might have been pleased that Julia had taken so much notice of what he was doing, but a man already on the defensive responded in kind. “Even if she was, why would I not consider the implications of it? She is a woman of the world after all.”

Julia pushed her chair back with force, then placed both hands on the table, leaning forward towards Hugh. She had never felt so angry in her life. “If occupying the beds of the likes of you and Mr Patrick qualifies her as a woman of the world, I can only rejoice that I am considered a dried-up spinster! Thank you for making yourself clear as to how you regard my friends and I, it has been most informative. If you will excuse me, I will speak to my uncle and we shall leave your house as soon as is practicable.”

“No! There is no need for this!” Hugh said, standing and moving around the table to stop Julia from leaving the room.

“You are mistaken in this, my lord. I feel there is every need.”

Hugh reached Julia and instead of pleading her forgiveness, he caught her arms, pulled her towards him and kissed her.

What he expected to happen at such brutish behaviour he would ponder later, but he certainly did not expect to land on the floor with an ungainly thud. Staring up at Julia, who towered over his prone form, he rubbed his chin. “Good God, woman, how did you manage to floor me?”

"Through many lessons from Gentleman Jackson, you absolute cad," Julia hissed at him.

Hugh collected himself and stood up but continued to rub his chin. "I am sorry, I should not have done that, I do not know what came over me. Please be assured that I have never forced a kiss on anyone before, I think I panicked at the thought of you leaving. You probably need ice on your knuckles," he babbled, wilting under Julia's stony glare.

She ignored the concerned glance he gave to her hand, which indeed was throbbing with pain, but looked at him with derision. "Am I to be flattered that I am the first woman that you were willing to disregard propriety and kiss? What possible madness would make you think that I wanted a kiss from you after our conversation?"

"Damn and blast it to the devil," Hugh cursed. "I have completely messed things up."

"That is an understatement."

"I have wanted to kiss you for at least the last month."

"As flattering as that might be to some, I suppose, it does not change the situation. You have managed to insult my friends and myself, and that is unforgivable. I will be leaving shortly. I shall let you explain to Florence why we have suddenly departed."

Hugh flopped down onto the nearest chair and held his head in his hands, not moving when the door opened some ten minutes later.

"Uncle, why are Julia and Uncle William returning to their own home? Uncle William seemed upset and Julia looks furious. I thought it best to leave her be and seek you out instead," Florence said.

"It is time for them to leave," Hugh answered.

"She hasn't turned you down when you offered for her, has she?"

Her words made Hugh look up. "What do you mean when I offered for her?"

"It is clear how smitten you are with each other," Florence shrugged. "I thought you were close to making a formal announcement."

"You see this chin?" Hugh asked, pointing to what he suspected was a rapidly developing bruise. "This is what I got when I acted like some bumbling Johnny Raw with Miss Marsh. Hence, they are leaving and I have not a clue how to make it right."

"You could start by apologising," Florence suggested before smiling mischievously. "What on earth did you do that caused Julia to punch you?"

"How do you know it was not Uncle William?"

"He is far too gentle a man to be so violent."

"That is not a good recommendation for Miss Marsh," came the dry response.

"Not at all. I know she will have suffered extreme provocation from you to have acted in such a way, dear uncle," Florence said.

"I cannot argue against that, and just so you know I did apologise, but it will not be enough. I overstepped the mark on more than one instance, and the insult I offered she rightly took offence to. I honestly do not know what I was thinking."

"Then you have some making up to do," Florence said.

"If only it was so simple."

"Do not be so defeatist, I know how well she thinks of you. Anyone can see it."

"That is the problem, someone did see it and determined they were going to cause mischief, and like the fool I am, I listened to them," Hugh responded. "I will not make that mistake again."

Chapter 17

John was shown into Hugh's study but paused at the door. "Good grief, man, what has happened?" he asked as he took in the state of his friend.

Frock coat cast aside, cravat loosened, ruffled hair due to pulling it and running his hands through it in frustration, Hugh looked up at his friend with sunken eyes. "Go away, John. I cannot wallow in a pit of despair if you are here."

"Thank goodness for that!" John said, entering the room. As he passed Richards, who was still standing just inside the door, he looked at him. "Tell his lordship's valet to expect his lordship soon. He is to work miracles because we are going out."

"No, I am not."

"Yes you are. I have left you to fester for long enough," John said, crossing the room to the decanters and pouring two glasses of brandy. "Here. Drink one of these and then we can get moving."

"I am not going anywhere, I have to stay here to protect Florence," Hugh mumbled, but gulped the brandy down.

"I counted seven footmen hanging around the hallway on my way to you, add that to your other staff and I am sure she will be well protected if you go out for an hour."

"Of course I will. I keep telling him to go out, but he is being stubborn," Florence said, entering the room. "One of us might as well escape this tedium."

"And that is supposed to encourage me to abandon you?" Hugh asked. "I have apologised a thousand times, and I have promised to take you to the theatre tonight."

"Perfect, and I will accompany you to the theatre for added protection," John said. "Now go and smarten yourself up, your valet is waiting."

Hugh moved out of the room and John raised his eyebrows at Florence. "Has he been like this since Miss Marsh and her uncle left?"

"Yes, he refuses to come out of this maudlin mood he has fallen into. Although I have visited Miss Marsh twice, and she does not seem to be any happier, but at least she looks presentable," Florence answered.

"I had left him alone for a few days, understanding that he would not want to be seen sporting a bruise, especially one given to him by a slip of a girl, but when I heard that he had not been to White's for over a week, I knew there was something amiss."

“It is what happens when you are in love, I suppose. Although I had thought it was supposed to be a happy time,” Florence said.

“All seems to be too much trouble to me,” John replied. “Better out of the marriage mart if it causes everyone to be so upset.”

“That is a very lonely way of looking at things.”

“As long as you have blunt in your pocket and clubs to go to, you can never be lonely.”

Florence shook her head at him. “Tell me you do not believe that is true? I might be young, Mr Carmichael, but I can assure you I have seen what happens when there is no family around you and you reach your dotage. No one helps, you are completely abandoned, it is sad to see.”

“Perhaps I will get married just before I reach my dotage then.” John laughed at Florence’s horrified expression. “I am teasing, Miss Weston. I want a happy marriage and a dozen brats just like the next man.”

“I really do need to work on reading people better,” Florence said. “Where I grew up people said what they meant, there was none of this saying one thing and doing another. It made life so much simpler.”

“I was funning with you.”

“There was never any time for funning, we were too busy trying to earn enough to eat.”

John looked horrified at his blunder. “I do beg pardon, Miss Weston.”

Florence laughed. "Perhaps I am better at this being in society thing than I give myself credit for," she said with a smile. "I was funning with you."

"She is a brat," Hugh drawled from the doorway, hair straightened, fresh cravat, waistcoat and frock coat. "Come, John, let me release you from this hoyden. Brat, I will be two hours. Everyone knows you are not to leave the house."

Florence sighed. "Yes, Uncle. I will lose myself in a novel for I refuse to do any more needlework. If I ever set up my own establishment, needlework will be prohibited."

John grinned at her before the two left. Florence settled into the morning room with a novel, bored but with no desire to venture out alone. The incident with the brick had unnerved her, and although knowing she could not hide forever, until Jack was caught, she was happy to remain surrounded by people who were determined to keep her safe.

Ten minutes after Hugh had left, Richards came to the door, a solemn expression on his face. "Miss Florence, there is a Mrs Ibbotson asking if you are at home."

"Is Mr Patrick with her?" Florence whispered to him.

"No, she is alone."

"Good. I wonder why she wants to see me? Please show her in."

"I think his lordship would prefer if you were to say you were not at home," Richards cautioned.

"Really? But why?"

Richards coughed, clearly embarrassed. "I think he would not like you associating with the likes of Mrs Ibbotson."

"But he introduced me to her," Florence said. "Please show her in, I have not had any female company these last few days and I am longing for a gossip."

"As you wish," Richards said before bowing and leaving the room.

Kathryn was shown into the morning room, looking with interest at everything around her. When she had seen enough, she smiled and reached out her hands to Florence in such an overt gesture of closeness that did not exist between the pair that it surprised the young girl.

"Miss Weston! I have missed seeing you this last week. I had to come and see that you were well and nothing was amiss when I heard that Miss Marsh had returned home. She has been absent from society too, but no one would have missed her, it was your absence that was commented on."

Florence had stiffened at the words but invited Kathryn to sit. "My uncle is waiting for the arrival of a distant cousin, and we could not keep Miss Marsh here forever."

"No, especially as I said to your uncle that people were starting to talk," Kathryn tinkled with a giggle quite out of place from a woman of her years.

"What about? Had they seen the same as I had, that my uncle and Miss Marsh would make a perfect match?" Florence knew she was speaking out of turn, but something about the predatory way Kathryn had assessed the room at her entrance and the way she was acting made Florence suspicious of her motives for visiting. In her own naïve way, she was endeavouring to warn Kathryn off because she wanted her uncle to marry Julia, but although an innocent in the ways of a woman like Kathryn, she was trying her best to divert her.

Florence saw the flicker of anger and jealousy the moment her words were uttered, and she suddenly thought that she had unintentionally made an enemy for Julia. Feeling more and more out of her depth, she waited to see how the woman would react.

"Not at all, your uncle would never be foolish enough to leg-shackle himself to a bluestocking. I know how much he values his reputation, and his friends would laugh at his choice," Kathryn responded.

"True friends would not," Florence said defensively.

"Miss Weston," Kathryn sighed. "I feel it is my duty to inform you a little about how society works. It is all about mixing with the right people, and the likes of

Miss Marsh, as pleasantly unassuming as she might be, can only cause you problems for you if you insist on being more than a passing acquaintance with her. If you want to be a diamond of the first water, you need to choose your friends carefully."

Florence could feel the tension in her face as she tried to keep her expression neutral, but she was struggling to hold her temper. "I would never consider Miss Marsh unassuming," she eventually said. "If you knew her better, you would understand that."

"I know you have been lost to your family for some years and have little experience of the types of people who make up society," Kathryn said sympathetically. "I am sure the Bluestockings have welcomed you with open arms into their little group, and who can blame them? Having you in their midst raises their credibility whilst at the same time reducing yours. Come, you are a young, vibrant woman. Tell me, sitting in meetings, discussing the latest handkerchief they have embroidered, cannot be the type of entertainment you would wish to enjoy?"

Florence laughed. "Goodness, no!"

"See, we are both of a similar mind," Kathryn said with a smile, confident now that she was getting her message across.

"We might be if that is what the meetings were about," Florence said with a gleam in her eyes, finally pleased that she had something to say that would show

Kathryn that the Bluestockings were not as staid as she accused them of being. "At one of the meetings, we were taught fencing techniques by none other than Mr Angelo himself. Miss Marsh arranged it. Perhaps she is not so unassuming after all?"

Kathryn's eyes narrowed. "You did what?"

"Mr Angelo was very good. Said if we needed protection from a ruffian accosting us in the street, we could use our parasols to defend ourselves." Florence had seen the change in Kathryn's posture, and although she had been triumphant in her ability to stop the snide comments about the meetings, she was now beginning to wonder if she had erred. Her mind was racing as to how she could recover the situation.

"You were fighting?"

"Only pretend fighting," Florence said, more uncomfortable by the second.

"How on earth did Miss Marsh arrange such a thing? Mr Angelo's time is very exclusive."

"Umm, I think she knows him." Florence tried not to squirm, but was not sure she was successful. "Should I ring for tea?"

"No, thank you," Kathryn said. "Who wants tea when you are being most enlightening?"

"I was only trying to prove to you that the meetings are interesting."

"They certainly sound it. I shall have to be far more circumspect whenever I am in the company of the Bluestockings in future. Who knew they were so dangerous? I can hardly believe it."

"They are all really nice."

"Spinsters who can fence! Next, you will tell me that they are having lessons from Gentleman Jackson." Kathryn was watching Florence like a hawk watching its prey before it plummets in for the kill.

"Er – no, there was some mention of him doing a talk, but I do not know if that will come to anything," Florence said, wishing she knew how to bring their meeting to an end without causing offence.

"And I suppose that would be arranged through Miss Marsh too?"

"I am not sure." But the tinge of colour on Florence's cheeks gave away the lie.

Kathryn leaned back in her seat. "Miss Weston, I think you are correct. It seems I have misjudged Miss Marsh completely, and she is not unassuming at all. I do beg your pardon."

"She is lovely and does so much to help people," Florence said eagerly, hoping the danger was over.

"I am sure she does. I suppose you wish to follow in her footsteps, getting to know the likes of Mr Angelo and Gentleman Jackson?"

"Oh no."

"I would have to wonder why she would need such people as friends. One could almost suspect that she was the one having the lessons from Gentleman Jackson. Oh, do not look so concerned, my dear; it has been common knowledge for a while that he has been giving lessons to a female. We have all been agog and desperate to find out who it could be, and now I know! It is the surprising Miss Marsh! Well, I never."

"Please do not reveal it is her, she has a valid reason for needing the lessons," Florence pleaded, trying desperately to control a situation that was so far out of control, her heart was pounding and her hands sweating.

"I would not do anything so uncharitable," Kathryn soothed. "But it is always useful to know about each other, is it not? Now tell me, is this the reason she has left? I cannot imagine that Hugh would tolerate someone acting as chaperone who is also frequenting men's clubs."

"Oh no, he has known about that from the start," Florence said guilelessly.

"Has he really? I am so glad that I visited today of all days," Kathryn said. "You are enlightening me in ways I can hardly believe."

"Why did you visit?" Florence asked, suddenly aware that it was probably no coincidence that Kathryn had visited on the day her uncle had gone out.

"As I said, to see how you were, for I have missed you at the parties I have attended."

"I am not out, I was never going to attend all the entertainments," Florence said.

"No, but neither do I. Those of us on the edges of society must stick together."

"Why are you on the edge of society?"

"Let's just say when you have no real fortune and your husband dies suddenly, you are forced to do things you would not normally consider, and society is not forgiving when that happens," Kathryn said, wiping a non-existent tear with her gloved finger.

"I am sorry," Florence said. "Have people treated you very poorly?"

"Some. I suppose I am more like your friends than I would care to admit, and perhaps I am a little jealous of them. They are tolerated by society no matter what they do, whereas I have to be very careful. Even your uncle has been a brute towards me."

"Uncle Hugh? Surely not?"

"Oh yes, he is not keen to let others see how he truly is, but he cast me off the moment his head was turned by Miss Marsh," Kathryn sighed.

"Cast you off? I do not understand. Were you engaged? Surely he would not be so cruel?"

"No, but we had an understanding," Kathryn confessed. "I thought he was the love of my life."

"Please forgive my ignorance and impertinence, but I am afraid I do not understand. I thought Mr Patrick was your beau? He seems very attentive,"

Florence said. She refrained from saying that she thought the man was slightly creepy and in no way compared to her uncle.

"Oh, he is extremely attentive, and he is a good friend, but how could I consider him when my heart is taken by his lordship?" Kathryn sighed. "I suppose I should not be so jealous of Miss Marsh, but she seems to have done nothing extraordinary, and yet he is besotted, although I now find out he approves of her strange antics."

"I would not go that far," Florence said. "He really did not want her going out on the streets at night, but her being there meant she was able to help us on the night we met."

"Oh really? How so?"

"We were being attacked and she helped," Florence said, unwilling to divulge anything more and unable to understand why she had just said what she had. She almost felt as if Kathryn was able to drag the words out of her before Florence had time to think about what she was saying. The young girl had no idea she was being manipulated by an expert.

"Obviously her lessons have paid off," Kathryn said easily. "I for one am glad that she was around late at night, alone, I presume? And able to help. No wonder she managed to grab your uncle's attention, she is clearly a paragon."

"She is very nice," Florence said, defeated.

"That much, along with everything else is very clear now," Kathryn said. "Now, tell me, Miss Weston, when are we to see you out?"

"We are attending the theatre tonight," Florence said. "My uncle has a box."

"He has. I enjoyed many evenings out with him there," Kathryn said. "You will have a lovely time, I am sure. Try and persuade your uncle to come to Mr Patrick's little soiree next week. I know he has received an invitation, but we have not had a reply as yet. There are just a select few of us, all good friends, it will be an informal gathering, but you would be most welcome."

"Thank you, I will ask him about it."

"Good girl. Right, I have taken up far too much of your time. I will leave you in peace, but I am so glad we have had our little chat. You have been most enlightening."

Florence's heart had lifted in relief that she had not caused as much damage to Julia as she feared, but once Kathryn's final words were uttered, she was thrown back into the depths of despair. She had been a fool and could only wonder how it would impact on Julia.

Chapter 18

William burst into the dining room, beetroot-faced, eyes wide. For a quiet, calm person, his whole demeanour was worrying.

"Uncle, what is it? Are you ill?" Julia stood immediately, all concern for her uncle.

"It has happened! Everything I feared has happened!"

"Come. Sit down. What are you talking about? Please tell me what is going on."

"This! This is what has happened! You are ruined!" William almost flung the paper at Julia.

With a sense of dread, she opened the paper, and on the third page, the headline screamed 'The Shadow's Identity Revealed!'.

She scanned the article, and when she reached the second line which read, *'We were all convinced that the saviour of the streets was a man, but we were fooled. Our source says that it was a spinster gentlewoman who has been patrolling our streets night after night and chasing away the criminal fraternity as if they were naughty schoolboys. How they must hang their heads in shame that a member of The*

Bluestocking Club, no less, could have us all fooled…' she sank into the seat she had just abandoned.

"Oh no," she said, continuing to read.

"I warned you," William said, pacing the room.

"But, Uncle, I have not been out since we moved in with Lord Weston. I promised I would not return to it and I did not," Julia defended herself.

"Others did! They took up the mantle of the shadow, and we have both read the reports day after day of the good deeds that have been happening. No one will believe that you have stopped."

"No one who knows me will believe it; it is too preposterous a claim to be convincing," Julia tried to persuade him.

"You have not been socialising since we left Lord Weston's home, yet every day there have been reports of the shadow at work. It will not take much to convince everyone that it was you."

"It was not."

"I know that, but they do not, and whoever revealed this has done you the worst possible damage in the eyes of society."

"The only people who knew about this were Lord Weston, Florence and Grace," Julia said. "I cannot believe one of them would reveal me." She wondered if Hugh would have. They had not parted on good terms, and though he was barely out of her thoughts, he could be seeking some form of revenge for the way she reacted when he kissed her. The thoughts had barely formed before she dismissed them. No. He would not be so vindictive.

Her musings were brought to an abrupt end when there was a banging on the door. "We are not at home!" William bellowed to an astounded servant who had never heard his employer raise his voice in the ten years he had worked for him.

Voices at the door became louder as Hugh marched into the dining room, a tearful Florence following him reluctantly.

"Oh no," Julia said, looking between Florence and Hugh. "Why?"

"It was Kathryn," Hugh said without preamble. "I am going to kill her when I get my hands on her."

"How did she find out? Did you...?"

"No, I did not!" Hugh ground out. "She bamboozled Florence into revealing most of the details and she probably guessed the rest; she is no fool and is an expert at getting what she wants."

"I am so sorry!" Florence sobbed. "I hoped she would forget what I had said, but I could hardly sleep last night, and then when I heard Uncle Hugh cursing, I knew she had done something horrible."

"Oh, Florence," Julia said.

"I am sorry, I do not know how I can make this right." She could barely get the words out, she was crying so hard.

"Come, stop this," Julia said, enfolding Florence into an embrace. "It is done, and it is I who took the risk, knowing what would happen if my activities were revealed."

"But nobody knew until Mrs Ibbotson started saying that there was nothing special about you and your friends, and Uncle would never marry someone like you," Florence continued to sob. "I just wanted to show her that you are amazing."

Julia was as white as a sheet, frown firmly in place, but she laughed at Florence's words. "Thank you. Perhaps next time, just let a bitter woman vent her spleen without trying to defend me."

"She said she was jealous of you."

"That is the biggest joke of all," Julia said. "Now come, there is nothing to be done. Perhaps we should leave town for a while, Uncle?"

"That would be running away," Hugh said.

"It would, but I cannot see a way back from this. I would rather not receive the cut direct from everyone at the next event I tried to attend."

Another knock at the door revealed that Grace was calling. When she was shown in, she approached Julia immediately. "This is what I feared."

"You and my uncle, both," Julia said wryly. "I have just suggested we leave town for an extended holiday."

"No!" Grace said. "You stay and convince everyone that the story is not true."

"But I revealed it to Mrs Ibbotson," Florence said.

"You should choose your liaisons more carefully, my lord," Grace said to Hugh. He looked as if to respond but instead just nodded silently.

"The newspaper obviously believed her, no one is going to take my word over hers," Julia said.

"You underestimate the power of the Bluestockings." Grace smiled. "We are all going out tonight and you will be there, surrounded by your friends. They will have to snub us all if they try to give you the cut direct."

"Grace, we are the spinsters who are the laughing stock of our society, do not try to convince me otherwise. Society will hardly care if one of us or all of us is given the cut direct," Julia said a little harshly.

"But you have friends," Hugh said. "We have let you down badly, but the perfect way to make it up to you is to give you our support. I will escort your group tonight, as will John and Florence. We will give the clear message that you are not friendless."

"You are not the only one with friends who will rally," Grace said. "We are not as desperate for connections as you would have us think, no one with money is a complete outcast. I will send notes out today, but I have already sent them to the girls. I would expect a steady stream of visitors this morning."

"What will they think when they know what I have been doing and that I did not tell them?" Julia asked.

"They will understand, although they might be a little hurt to start with. We all have secrets, Julia, no one is completely honest with each other."

"That has my curiosity piqued." Julia smiled at her friend.

"It will have to stay that way." Grace smiled in return. "Which party are we going to show a united front at?"

"It is not really appropriate for Florence to attend, but there is the Thursbys' ball being held tonight," Hugh said.

"That is perfect, it will be the largest gathering this evening. I think Miss Weston should be allowed to attend as a one-off. After all, if my scheme does not go to plan, it will be a very short attendance." Grace smiled. "Do not look so worried, Julia, I am funning with you. All will be well."

"I wish I had your confidence," Julia said.

"I am determined that you will not be ruined because of this. Now excuse me, I have to go and rally our friends." Grace left the room, intent on her mission.

Hugh approached Julia. “Could I have a private word, please?”

“As you wish,” Julia said, reluctantly leading the way out of the dining room and into the drawing room.

Hugh waited until they were in the room before turning to Julia. “I am truly sorry for everything that has happened. I have been played like a fool by a woman who I should never have been with in the first place. Even then, I was foolish, allowing her flattery to persuade me into starting something I should have run away from. Fast.”

“This is not some sort of confessional, my lord,” Julia said stiffly.

“No. I am just trying to explain, badly, that I have made a number of huge mistakes. But I cannot be completely sorry about them because some of my actions brought me to you, and I will never regret that.”

Julia walked to the fireplace and, picking up the poker, roughly stabbed the smouldering coals. Waiting until she felt calm enough to speak, she turned to face Hugh. “I cannot do this anymore,” she said simply.

“Do what?”

“Listen to you speak about another woman who you have been intimate with. I am sorry, my lord. I do not wish to hear another word about you and her. I am foolish in that it affects me so much, but I will not torture myself further,” she said, meeting his gaze.

"You have feelings for me," Hugh said, a smile forming on his lips.

"It does not matter what I feel," Julia said, dashing Hugh's hopeful expression. "I cannot allow myself to continue in this vein. We are not suited, the past weeks have proved that."

"I do not see how," Hugh said, his mind racing as to how the situation seemed to be spiralling quickly out of his control and not in a good way.

"The only time you attempted to kiss me was when you were angry with me. That is not a good sign in any way it is examined."

"That was an error on my part and one I am ashamed of," Hugh said. "But it was because I have wanted to kiss you since the first night we met. I have been desperate for the opportunity or the courage to kiss you since that night."

"You thought I was a man!"

"I did not. The way you walked convinced me that you were every bit a woman, and when I grabbed you, my theory was confirmed."

Julia flushed red. "Yet you gave no indication that you were attracted to me and have never done so though we were living under the same roof."

"It was exactly that reason that I could not do anything," Hugh responded quickly. "I could not take advantage of you while you were acting the chaperone, yet I did not want to employ anyone else because that would take you away from me, and I did not want that either."

"This is too confusing. Do you realise what you are saying?"

"Let me put it in simple terms. When I first met you, I was intrigued, wanted to kiss you. Then I wanted to make sure you were safe; the thought of you being in danger terrified me, but then my arrogance was repaid by you rescuing me." He smiled at her. "I knew I was attracted to you, and John has complained that I have become quite the home bird since you moved in. The reason was I wanted to be at home, I needed to spend every moment I could with you, but then it hit me. I did not like you, I loved you and probably had from the start, only the fool that I am, I had not realised it. Not surprising really when you look at the parents I had. I had not known what love was until I met you, and now because of me you are going to suffer further, and I need you to tell me how to put it right."

Julia was stunned by the long speech, but the sentiment and the feeling behind the words touched her deeply. She grimaced. "It has been torture having that woman around. Constantly glaring at us and watching you like you were hers and hers only."

"She cannot compare to you in any way, and if you give me the chance to make everything right, I solemnly promise that you will never need to feel that way about anyone again. I will be yours in body and soul."

"Those are very serious promises," Julia said.

"I would only ever make them to you. I have only ever wanted to make them to you, no one else I have ever met can compare to you. I hope you believe how strongly I feel."

"It is not a good time for your declaration," Julia said. "You want to protect me; you have the urge to provide security for those you care about, but think of it from my point of view. I would hate to think that an association with me would cause you to suffer by being snubbed by your friends."

"They could rot in hell for all I care. If they do not accept you as my wife, then they are not worth being in the same company."

"Is that what you want?" Julia asked. Her mind could barely keep up with how the day was turning out. She had gone from being horrified and afraid that she would be cast out, to having an offer made from the man of her dreams. She could hardly believe it and had to be sure that he was sincere; she would not be able to agree to any help from him if he was doing it purely out of obligation. "I need to know that you are sure about what you are asking."

"More than I have been sure about anything else in my life. Can you forgive my blunders, arrogance, and the fact that my niece has inadvertently revealed your secret to the world?"

"You aren't offering your hand as some sort of peace offering, are you?" Julia asked, suddenly suspicious of his motives.

"Of course I am not!" Hugh spluttered. "For God's sake, woman, most would rejoice at my proposing to them, instead you throw it back into my face! What can I do to convince you that I am in earnest, apart from to say that if you refuse me, I will never offer for another woman? After all, there cannot be two of you in the world; there can only be one annoying, frustrating, challenging, funny woman sent to test me."

Laughing, Julia crossed the room to him. "I just wanted to be sure you were doing it for the right reasons. I have never seen you hanging around the Bluestockings before, so I should quite rightly be suspicious of your motives."

"My motive is to marry you at the earliest opportunity, and then you can torment me for the rest of my days, you termagant," Hugh said. "Now will you please say yes, so that I can kiss you? This time because you want to be kissed. I will never be so foolish as to force a kiss on you ever again, it was too painful."

"Yes. Kiss me, you fool."

Chapter 19

When they eventually separated, Julia rested her hand on Hugh's shoulder. She had enjoyed running her hands through his hair while she had been kissed thoroughly and was reluctant to completely pull away from him. "Can I ask one thing of you?"

"With kisses like that, you can ask anything," Hugh said, giving her butterfly kisses as he spoke.

"Can we make an announcement when all the furore over the article dies down?" Julia asked.

"Why? Surely it would help to take everyone's minds from that to the engagement and then the wedding. You know how everyone loves a good wedding."

"It might, but it also could lead people to believe it is some sort of ploy for us to deflect attention. I am six and twenty and thought my chance at marriage had passed. Instead, I have met a man I want to spend the rest of my days with, and I would like to enjoy every part of the preparations for that," Julia tried to explain. She wanted to hide from society but knew that she could not.

"I can see your point. I had just hoped that we could be married soon. Very soon."

Julia looked at Hugh with renewed suspicion. "This distant cousin of yours, does she actually exist?"

"I do have distant cousins," Hugh started.

"You terror! You want a quick marriage so that I continue to be Florence's chaperone! Admit it!"

"I will admit nothing of the sort," Hugh laughed, unable to stop himself from kissing her again. "That it is an unlooked-for advantage and is purely coincidental."

"You rogue of rogues. I can see I am going to have to watch you. But no, I will not get married just yet," Julia said.

"Fine, if you insist. Promise me one thing, though," Hugh said, turning serious.

"What?"

"Let us tell our family and close friends. I do not want any more secrets. The rest of society can be damned, but I want those we hold close to be a party to the secret, for them to be as pleased as I am at the news."

"That I can agree with," Julia said.

"Thank you. Let us join the others and break the news," Hugh said. Taking hold of her hand, he led the way out of the room and back to their family.

***

Julia had never been so nervous as she prepared for the ball that evening. All her Bluestocking friends had visited her during the day, apart from Arabella, who was almost a hermit and lived away from the capital. Even Lydia had called, who had been out of town visiting a property she had suddenly inherited. Alice was staying with her and they had both travelled to show their support. Julia had been very touched. All her Bluestockings had offered their support, but had also quizzed Julia as to what she had done, amazed that she had risked so much for others.

Feeling drained from the emotional day she had gone through, she would have far rather crawled into bed and hidden from those she now had to face, but she had to attend the ball, delaying it would not achieve anything. If she hid away from everyone, she would not know whether she had been cast out or not.

Uncle William had tried to persuade her to announce her engagement, but she had remained steadfast. No announcement until after everything else had settled down. That she had decided if she was an outcast, she would release Hugh from the engagement and try to live without him, she had not confessed to anyone, but she could not keep him bound to her if she was ostracised. If she had to break off their secret engagement, it would be far harder than facing a ballroom full of critical people. She grimaced at the thought whilst watching herself in the looking glass as her hair was being dressed.

She had experienced the greatest joy and the depths of despair in the same day and could not predict how the evening was going to end.

One thing was for sure, she was in love with Hugh, so much that it almost took her breath away, and she had never been happier to find out that he felt the same. She had felt a pang, wishing her parents were alive to see her finally meet a man who was her equal in all regards, but if they had been alive, she would probably never have met him. Strange how life turned out, she mused as her maid finished curling the tendrils that framed her face.

Walking downstairs some fifteen minutes later, she was touched to see Uncle William, Hugh, Florence and John all gathered at the foot of the stairs.

"Are you afraid I would run away if you were not here to escort me?" she asked Hugh.

"Most certainly," he said with a slight bow. "You look lovely, I wish I could tell everyone that you have agreed to be mine."

"Thank you, and we will announce it soon, let us get this over with first," she sighed.

"We are to arrive a little later than normal," Hugh said.

"Why? I do not think it is a good idea to make a grand entrance, tonight of all nights," Julia said, her apprehension increasing.

"I forewarned the Thursbys," Hugh started. "They might not be titled, but they hold a lot of sway in society. Remember what happened when the Duchess of Yarnton took it upon herself to reveal her son was not hers at one of their balls? She might have been a duchess, but when the Thursbys sided with the duke who had tried to make things right in a bad situation, everyone followed the lead that the Thursbys took. It was the right thing to do, and it shows what sway they have in society."

"And you have begged them to show me support?" Julia said. She was not happy that people were being forced into supporting her.

"Not at all. When I spoke to Thursby, he called his wife in and told her the tale. She said that she had been close friends with your mother when they were children, but they had drifted apart as some people do. She was completely supportive of you, I did not need to beg at all." Hugh grinned at her.

"I knew they were friends. Mrs Thursby has mentioned it over the years, but I had not realised they were close," Julia said. "She has always been very friendly and considerate to me. I suppose I should have guessed."

"Your parents were well liked everywhere they went," William said quietly. "That will stand you in good stead now, my child."

"I am so very sorry to have put you through all of this, Uncle," Julia said, crossing to kiss him on the cheek.

"I understood it was something you had to do. I am just glad it is at an end."

"It most certainly is," Julia responded. "Come. I cannot stand to wait around any longer, the waiting is almost as scary as the event itself. Let us leave."

Hugh moved and got hold of Julia's hand, bringing it to his lips and kissing it. "I will be by your side every step of the way."

"Thank you," Julia said. Her throat had constricted at his words, but she would not show weakness, even to those she loved. "Lead on, my lord. We have a ball to attend."

***

On entering the hallway, Julia laughed to see her gaggle of Bluestockings waiting in the foyer for her to arrive.

Grace crossed to her. "We are ready to join you in battle whenever you are."

"I am so very thankful for your support, but I do not wish you all to be ostracised too," Julia said not for the first time that day.

"Tsk, society is overrated," Serena said. "If I am given the cut direct, it will give me the reason to finally leave these shores and go and explore the world."

Julia kissed her friend. "I am sick of telling you, you should do it anyway."

"One day." Serena smiled. "Let me see you happily settled in society first, oh and I must wait to attend the wedding of course."

Hugh had never left Julia's side and now whispered to her. "I think it is time to make that entrance."

Julia looked at him and set her shoulders. "It is."

The group fell into step behind Hugh and Julia, who led the way into the ballroom. A large group arriving at once would always gather some curious looks from those near the entrance to the ballroom, but Julia's party heard the ripple as the news of their arrival flowed through the large room.

A silence descended, the only noise coming from the quartet playing on the other side of the room and the dancers too engrossed in their activity to notice anything amiss.

Julia had never had so many eyes on her at once, and her heart pounded as she waited for the first person to turn their back on her, giving her the cut direct. It was like waiting to be tortured, and all she wanted to do was turn tail and run from the house.

When she thought her courage was faltering, Mr and Mrs Thursby appeared at her side and Mrs Thursby grasped both her hands. "You brave, brave girl!" she exclaimed. "Your parents would be so proud of you, and to think whilst we were all wasting our time, dancing our evenings away, you were out there protecting us! How can we ever thank you?"

"I-I did it because of the way my parents were taken," Julia stuttered. "I could not stand to see anyone else die in the same way." Mrs Thursby's words caused her to reveal more than she usually would and never in such a public way.

"You poor dear! You were so young when it happened. I still miss your mother, and I know she would be so impressed, as we all are." Mrs Thursby waved her arm in the general direction of the partygoers. "We need to know how you managed to persuade Mr Jackson to give you lessons. I suspect you will be able to give most of the gentlemen here some pointers, for I do believe he was very impressed with your ability."

Mr Thursby laughed. "On that note, let me take you to the Duke of Richmond. You saved his niece some months ago, and he wants to thank you."

Mr Thursby took hold of Julia's hand and put it on his arm, leading the way through the crowd. The group left behind could hear his voice booming across the room as he walked, praising Julia and asking her all sorts of questions as they weaved through the people, who were still watching with interest.

Hugh gave his companions a wry smile while everyone in the room returned to their own groups as Julia and Mr Thursby passed them, clearly talking about Julia. But she had not been cast out as her family and friends had feared. "That is the first hurdle over. Now for the rest of the evening. Good luck, everyone; go and work your magic."

The group split apart as previously agreed and each went to the people they knew, talking about the amazing Julia and the feats of bravery she had carried out.

It was half an hour before Hugh approached Kathryn and Mr Patrick. He had purposely kept away from her initially, even though he had wanted to throw her out of the ball the moment he had seen that she was there. Now he decided it was a good thing that Kathryn had attended. Everyone rallying around Julia would have given Kathryn a clear message. He was now about to prevent anything else from occurring in the future, he would not allow Julia to suffer any more because of his foolishness.

"I should not be surprised at your attending tonight," he drawled at Kathryn. As he stood to the side of her, he wondered what he had ever seen to attract him. She looked mean-spirited and sour-faced, the complete opposite of Julia, who was no fool but had a sense of fun and devilry that shone through. At first glance, one would always say that Kathryn was the prettier, but there was something about Julia that was far more appealing. Hugh realised that it was the whole package; she was handsome, good, intelligent and feisty, and he loved every aspect of her person. "After all, you would want to see the result of your interference. Tell me, did the newspaper pay you well? I hope so, for I think you are going to struggle to find favour in the future from the more sensible ones around you."

"I have no idea what you are referring to, my lord. If you are jealous that I abandoned your puppy love to a man more worthy of my attentions, please do not make yourself look foolish by making a scene," Kathryn responded lightly, but she was watchful and clearly annoyed that Julia was being paraded from group to group by Mr Thursby.

Hugh threw his head back and laughed. "Jealous? Me? That is a fine one for someone who was so jealous of a woman ten times the person she is that you went to the newspapers to try and damage her reputation."

"What the devil are you talking about?" Mr Patrick intervened. "Kathryn has done nothing of the sort."

"I think you will find she has done exactly what I accuse her of, have you not?" Hugh asked Kathryn.

Kathryn shrugged. “Everyone wanted to know who the shadow was, I have let them know. What is wrong with that?”

“There is a lot wrong with that,” Mrs Thursby said, appearing at Hugh’s side. “We do not embarrass one of our own who has done no wrong,” she continued. “By revealing Miss Marsh’s secret, you have put her at risk from every fool who will want to challenge the shadow. I do not appreciate that you would willingly put a young woman in such a position. At your age, you should know better.”

“How dare you! She is nothing but an outcast, but because she has money you are siding with her!” Kathryn spat.

“She has far more than money,” Mrs Thursby said, completely unruffled at the venom oozing from Kathryn. “She has class, something which no matter how much you try, or who you persuade to escort you about town, you will never have. Mr Patrick, I think your *partner* needs to go home, and please let me offer you some advice, do not bring her out again. She will not be welcome.”

It was clear that Mr Patrick was mortified at what Mrs Thursby was saying. He looked at Kathryn and patted her arm. “Best you go home now,” he said.

“What? You are not escorting me?” Kathryn asked.

"I think it best not to. I will stay here and I'll send a note around tomorrow. Best go quietly," Mr Patrick said, stepping back from Kathryn.

She turned to Hugh. "You have not heard the last of this," she hissed at him.

"You need to learn to admit when you have made a mistake," Hugh said. "You crossed the wrong people and there are consequences to that."

"She will never satisfy you as I did!" Kathryn snapped before turning on her heel and storming from the room.

Hugh had watched Kathryn as she departed, suffering no pang of guilt that she would not be welcome in his circle any longer. Her actions had brought the ire of those around her onto herself, but his satisfaction was short-lived when he saw that Julia was close enough to have heard Kathryn's parting shot to him.

He knew it was vitriol from a bitter woman who knew she was losing her income from the men who provided for her whilst they favoured her, but Julia was still an innocent in many respects. Without them having the conversation, he was aware she would be worried about the intimate side of their marriage, and it was plain to see that Kathryn had scored a hit with her words.

Julia stood stock still, tears in her eyes, and Hugh decided that a grand gesture was needed.

Striding to her, he scooped her into his arms and kissed her soundly in front of everyone.

There were shocked gasps at his audacity, but when he looked up at the crowd, a cheeky grin on his face and said, “I am just making you all aware that this amazing woman is taken,” the room erupted into laughter and applause.

Lifting Julia back to a standing position, he kissed her gently. “I wanted to make sure you and the world know that you are the only person I could ever love,” he said quietly.

“But what she said—” Julia started, but Hugh put his finger on her lips.

“If your kisses are anything to go by, she is wrong, very wrong,” he whispered, a devilish smile touching his lips.

Julia flushed deep red. “You can sweet talk me too easily. I am going to spend my whole time befuddled when you are around.”

“In that case, we shall make a fine pair because that is how I have felt since I first met you. Now, will you please let me announce our engagement, for I am completely ruined after tonight’s show.”

“Yes, you rogue, go ahead,” Julia said.

“She said yes!” Hugh shouted to the room, which prompted more cheers and applause.

Embracing Julia once more, he smiled at her. “I promise to make you smile like this every day.”

"Even when I am tormenting you?" she asked archly.

"Especially then."

Chapter 20

Florence had never been happier. She spent half her time with an uncle, who although still seemed slightly intimidating, she knew loved her, and the rest of her time she spent with Julia or William. Wedding planning was exciting, but she also loved to work with William in his work room.

The news of Julia's exploits had resulted in a surge of orders for the canes he had made for a few members of the *ton*. Now, it seemed that everyone wanted one, and Florence happily carried out some of the smaller tasks to help speed up production.

"Does your uncle realise that you are going to want your own inventing room soon?" Julia asked Florence when the young woman had joined her after a busy afternoon.

"I find it fascinating watching how Uncle William puts the mechanism together," Florence confessed. "I could watch him for hours."

"You do," Julia teased.

"Time just passes in the blink of an eye when I am with him."

"He enjoys your company just as much," Julia said.

"Do you think he will join us when we go to the country house?"

"I am not sure. He always lived alone until I was thrust upon him," Julia said. "I have said that we would love to have him stay, even provide a workshop for him, but I get the impression that he would prefer to remain here."

"I suppose he has so much business now, he should make the money while he can."

"You are not only an apprentice to him, you are turning into a businesswoman as well! Your uncle will curse me to the devil if I do not make sure that you are a fine lady by the time you have your come out next season."

Florence grimaced. "I think my experience this year should convince my uncle that I should be permanently sent to the country."

"It has all worked out in the end."

"There has been no news about Jack, though," Florence said.

"I know. I am hoping that he thinks you are so well protected that you are not worth the bother."

"I hope so, but I will be happier when we leave London. I constantly feel as if I am being followed, but I know it is just my imagination."

"Have you seen anything to make you think that way?" Julia asked, immediately on the alert.

"No, it is just a feeling. I check behind me, but there is never anyone there. I have even had the footmen check the area a time or two, but they found nothing to have caused my worry. I suppose I am just too sensitive."

"Rather be like that than find yourself in a situation in which you are in danger," Julia said. "The footmen have been employed for their bulk and ability, they will protect you."

"I now feel like the princess Ma was considered to be, always being followed by servants. It has been a very strange few months."

"For us both," Julia agreed. "Thankfully, both of our lives are the better for what has happened."

"They are. I suppose it is time to go, I have to fit in a piano lesson before the theatre tonight."

The women embraced before Florence was escorted out. Julia watched from the window until the carriage was out of sight. She hoped it was just an overactive imagination on Florence's part, but she scrutinised every alleyway that she could see, looking out for anything unusual. Ten minutes later, she moved away from the window, happy at least that Florence had not been followed from Half Moon Street.

***

Florence dabbed her eyes, leaning away from the front of the box. "I thought this was supposed to be a comedy," she whispered to Julia as she wiped the tears away.

Julia smiled at her. "You are becoming a big softy, it is not so sad."

The curtain dropped, and refreshments were served in a room at the rear with the other members of the boxes. It was more intermingled than Hugh preferred, but that was the design of the theatre, so he had to pretend to be sociable during the intervals, which he was teased about by his niece and his betrothed.

Florence closed her eyes as she ate her third fancy. "These are so good," she mumbled around the food.

"Be careful, brat, or you will need a whole new wardrobe of clothes if you carry on eating dozens of those cakes," Hugh said, taking his own bite of the soft sponge encased in icing and piped decoration.

Florence grinned. "I would eat dozens if I thought no one would notice."

"Me too," Hugh said, mirroring her look of contentedness as he ate the cake.

"I wonder if I could get the recipe so that Cook could make some?" Florence mused.

"Do you think that is a good idea?" Hugh asked, starting on his second.

"If she only baked them once a week, we would not become too fat."

"I can feel my waist expanding with every bite," Hugh groaned.

"Please let me ask one of the waiters to take me to the manager and ask how I can get the recipe. I would like Cook to make them for you, it is the least I can do for everything you have done for me," Florence said.

"I wanted to make things right," Hugh admitted.

"And you have, and this can be my thank-you."

"By making me portly?"

"Old relatives always get fat," Florence said, giggling at the horrified expression on Hugh's face.

"Old?" he spluttered.

"I will be back soon." She waved cheerfully, leaving the box whilst Hugh shook his head with a smile on his face.

Julia returned to Hugh's side when the interval was over, she had been chatting to some acquaintances. "I wonder when the story of my being the shadow will get old?" she asked with a sigh as they returned to their box.

"It will need something else to happen first. What are you complaining about? You are infamous,"

Hugh responded, still holding one of the cakes in his hand.

"I like attention just as much as you do," Julia responded dryly.

"You are far better than me at handling the adoration of your public."

"That is because you glower at everyone. Where is Florence?" Julia asked.

"She went to get the recipe for these cakes," Hugh answered.

"You two and those fancies! I missed them this time, they had all gone by the time I escaped the Hunters. I hope she gets the recipe, I feel cheated that I have not had any. Unless, of course, you give me that one in your hand right there."

Hugh smiled at her. "I will ask Cook to make them tomorrow, just for you, but you are not having this one."

"I could still change my mind about our marriage," Julia said.

"You would not."

"Do you want to test that by eating every crumb of that fancy?"

"Oh, blast it," Hugh moaned. "I cannot eat it now, with you looking at me with those eyes. You are like a sad puppy."

"I think you need to work on your endearments, and just think, I have saved you from being a portly groom on our wedding day." Julia moved quickly, leaning forward and taking a chunk out of the cake still being held by Hugh.

He laughed, causing a few people in the theatre to stare at them, but his attention was on Julia. "You wretch," he growled before kissing her, all thought of cake forgotten.

After a further fifteen minutes, Hugh gazed around the theatre, and not seeing what he was looking for, he moved to the back of the box, with Julia following him.

"I am getting concerned, she should be back by now," he said as explanation for leaving the box. "I am going to check with the waiters to see where she went."

"I will remain here in case she returns," Julia said, looking around, half expecting Florence to appear at any moment.

Within half an hour it was clear that Florence was not in the building. Hugh was beside himself with worry, and the footmen who had remained with the carriage had been sent out to search the streets surrounding the theatre in case there was any sign of her.

"I let my guard down," Hugh said, pacing in the now empty refreshment room at the rear of the boxes.

"It is not unreasonable to think she was safe in a theatre full of people," Julia said, but she was feeling as distressed as Hugh.

"I should have thought it through, anyone can come into a theatre. Any number of Jack's men could have been in the stalls," Hugh said.

The footmen returned, breathless and looking concerned. "My lord," the first footman said, holding out a piece of torn material. "This was on the stage door."

"It is from her dress," Julia said.

"I need to go and find her," Hugh said.

He turned away as if to leave the building, but Julia put her hand on his arm. "Wait, I am coming with you. We need to be prepared. Going off without deciding what needs to be done will put us all in danger; we need to be armed and go in as one."

"I cannot put you at risk."

"You know I can be a useful asset, so stop talking nonsense. We need footmen, dressed to fight if necessary, and an express sent to Bow Street. We need as much help as we can get," Julia said.

Hugh nodded in agreement, and they left the theatre together.

***

Florence cursed to herself as the carriage she had been thrown into trundled through the streets of London. She had no way of knowing where she was; having a sack thrust over her head blocked her senses enough to not know which direction she was travelling in.

She was cursing her own stupidity; the first rule of survival was to trust your instincts, and she had dismissed hers as being oversensitive. Jack's henchmen being in the theatre was no coincidence, she had thought she was being followed, now she knew she had been.

She dreaded seeing Jack, for he was a violent man, she could only imagine what he would do to her when they finally met. A shudder went through her when she thought of him forcing himself on her; she would be ruined in the most brutal way.

The carriage came to a halt, and Florence had to struggle not to cast up her accounts through fear. Swallowing the bile, she was roughly dragged out of the carriage, her legs scratched against the rough ground and scraped on the steps. As she cried out in pain, she was slapped across the head and told to be quiet.

Doing as she was bid, even though her legs smarted and bled, she partially walked and was partly dragged into a building. When she was thrown onto a chair, the sack was removed and she tried to blink to see where she was and who faced her.

“Hello, Jack,” she croaked out, refusing to let him see how afraid she was.

“Well, well, well, the spawn of the princess has returned to her roots. I’ve been waiting a long time to see you again. We have some unfinished business to attend to.” The short, stocky man smiled, but his eyes held a look of pure menace.

Florence met his gaze and could hold back no longer. Leaning forward in the chair, she was violently sick, which made Jack jump back in disgust.

Chapter 21

Julia had insisted on changing her dress. "I cannot fight if I am encumbered by my skirts," she argued. "We also need supplies from Uncle William, so it is not out of our way to call at Half Moon Street."

Hugh reluctantly agreed. She was right, but every moment he was not searching felt like a moment lost. He had to find her, he had promised to protect her and had let his guard down; he was furious with himself.

The moment Julia entered the house at Half Moon Street, she was surprised to see a maid and her uncle waiting for her. The maid approached her. "Miss Marsh, I was told to give you this note the moment you came in. He said it was urgent you read it before you did anything else."

"Who said? Who delivered it?" Hugh demanded as Julia tore open the seal and read the missive.

"A young delivery boy, sir," the maid answered. "I asked him why it was so urgent, and he said he'd been given a clip around the ear for asking the same question. He begged me to give it to Miss Marsh. I've not dared to leave the hallway."

"We have both been eager for your return. I was tempted to open the letter, but thought it could only be to do with either the newspaper article or Miss Florence and did not wish to cause any more problems than was necessary," William said.

"Florence has been taken from the theatre," Hugh said.

William sucked in a breath and the maid helped him to sit on a chair. "The poor child," William moaned to himself.

Julia had gone pale whilst reading the note but screwed it into a ball, putting her hand at her side. "This note offers her safe return. I have to send a message confirming we will supply what they want," she said.

"What are they asking for?"

"M-money," Julia said, not quite meeting Hugh's gaze.

"I can get money. How much do I need? Let me look at the note."

"There is no need," Julia said quickly. "You get a hundred pounds and I will wait here for you. The handover will occur here."

Hugh frowned at her. "Here, why? And why are they asking for so little money? I would expect ten times as much."

"He will have chosen here because he probably thinks we will not have as many servants as you do."

"I will bring them back with me. I will happily pay far more for her return, but if I can get hold of the cur—"

"You are wasting time. Be gone and return soon," Julia said.

Hugh kissed her on the lips quickly before leaving the house. William looked at his niece before dismissing the maid.

"What does it really say, Julia?" he asked.

"They will swap Florence for the shadow. Nothing else. And if there is a delay, or if I do not go alone, she will be killed immediately," Julia said. "I need to go and change. If they want the shadow, that is what they will get."

"No! Julia, you cannot!" William cried, standing to try to stop his niece.

"I can, and I am going to. I will not have someone else killed because of my actions," Julia said.

"What on earth do you mean?"

Julia sighed, hating that she was wasting time, but she owed her uncle an explanation so that he could perhaps understand her reasoning. "Mother and Father were not going to go out that evening, I had been unwell, but I persuaded them to go. If they had done as they had wished, they would still be alive today."

"Oh Julia, it was not your fault. They took a walk, which was completely out of character for them, and then your father tried to outwit the robbers instead of just handing everything over and getting out of there. You had no control over any of that," William said.

"I do have some responsibility over what happened. They wanted to stay with me, I told them to go," Julia said. "I refuse to risk anything happening to Florence because of my actions, or lack of them. Please, I have to change before Hugh returns." She paused as she took the first step of the stairs. "If I should not be able to get away, please try and make him understand," she said before running up the stairs so that William could not see her anguish, for he would try to use it to persuade her to stay, and she could not do that.

Leaving the house only ten minutes later, Julia ran through the streets. She had never run along the streets so early in the night, and although her feet did not make a sound on the pavement, she no longer cared who saw her. All that mattered was to rescue Florence.

Approaching the meeting point, she immediately saw the gathering. They were not trying to hide, which worried her. She could only hope that when Florence was released, she would be able to get to safety.

Walking confidently to the two men who held Florence, and the man she guessed was Jack, she tried not to show the concern she felt for her. Florence was being held up, her dress was torn, and she was tear-stained.

"You had better not have hurt her," Julia snarled, completely immersed in the character she had to play.

Jack laughed. "The chit can't stop casting up her accounts. I thought I was going to have a good time with her before I sent her back, but you'll have to do instead. You're not as pretty but you'll do."

"I am here now, let her go." She suppressed a shudder at what she would face; she had to remain strong or she would never be able to escape.

"I am waiting for the signal," Jack said. After a few minutes of silence, in which the only sound was when Florence started to retch, a whistle was heard from across the park.

Jack nodded to the two men holding Florence, and they stepped back, releasing her. As she crumpled to the ground, Julia ran forward to lift her up. Shaking Florence, she whispered urgently to her, "Florence, you have to move or this will have been for nothing."

Florence started to cry. "I can't move. I am so afraid."

Julia shook Florence roughly. "Look at me!" she demanded. When she had Florence's attention, she continued. “You are going to get up and run like you have never run before. Uncle William is waiting for you, and your uncle will be there by the time you return. I need you to look after him, do you understand me?”

Florence looked at her in horror. “You think you won’t come back!”

“If I can, I will, but you must get to them and be their comfort. I need to know you will be safe.” Julia passed something small into her hand, and when Florence looked in surprise at the knife sheathed in her palm, Julia spoke. “Use it to get home safe if you need to. Now go!”

Julia almost pushed Florence away and only turned back towards Jack when the sound of Florence’s footsteps had disappeared.

“We have unfinished business,” Jack said. “I do not forget when someone bests me, especially a woman. You are going to suffer for your interference in every way I can think of. And I have a very active imagination.”

***

Hugh knew the moment he walked through the door on Half Moon Street that she was not there, without the fact that William dashed towards him in a blind panic. It had taken them slightly longer than anticipated to return because John had wanted his pistols.

"What the devil has happened?" Hugh demanded.

"She lied about the note!" William cried.

"Damn it! Tell me the full story."

"The man who has Florence does not want money, he wanted Julia – the shadow. She said she could not risk Florence's life by everyone turning up and so has gone to meet them," William babbled.

"Where?"

"I do not know. She would not let me see the note, just ran upstairs, changed into her outfit and then was off. You must follow her!"

Hugh started to run up the stairs. "Which is her chamber?" he shouted as he ran.

"The third door on the left," William replied.

Bursting into the room, Hugh took no notice of anything other than what he hoped Julia had left. If she had taken the note with her, they would have no chance of working out where she had gone. Cursing under his breath, he scanned the room. He had to find her.

Just as he was about to give up, a crumpled piece of paper caught his eye in the fireplace. The fire was set but not lit, and she had clearly thrown it there, knowing that at some point soon the maid would light the fire and all evidence of the note would be lost.

“Thank God you were in a hurry,” Hugh muttered to himself. If she had felt like she had more time, she would have probably lit the fire herself.

Scanning the note, he immediately ran back to the stairs, taking them two at a time. “She has gone to Green Park, the first crossroads in the wooded area.”

The party had turned to go out of the house when the door burst open and Florence ran in as if the devil himself were after her.

Flinging herself into William’s arms, letting go of the knife which she had clung to since Julia had given it to her, she sobbed as it clattered to the floor. “I did not want to leave, but she said I had to,” she wailed.

“Florence, are you hurt?” Hugh demanded.

“No, I am well. Please get to her. Jack is in a foul mood, I do not know what he is going to do,” Florence said between tears.

“Come on, there is no time to lose. If they move from the park, we will never find them. William, look after Florence and for God’s sake lock yourself in!” Hugh said, running out of the house.

The sight of footmen, a lord and his friend all running towards Green Park would not be seen by many, but quite a few of the residents of Half Moon Street would comment that their sleep had been disturbed by a strange thudding noise as many footsteps thundered along the street.

"I have got to find her," Hugh muttered to himself as he pummelled the pavement with his feet. The thought of what she could be facing sent a cold shiver down his spine; it was clear Jack wanted to make an example of the shadow. He was certain that Florence would never be safe whilst Jack was at large. He had no idea why Florence had been released, he was just thankful she had been and seemed to be unhurt.

He could only hope the same was true of Julia.

Chapter 22

Julia was as aware as Hugh was that if she was taken from Green Park, any chance of a rescue would be slim to none. Although outnumbered, she had to try to delay them leaving. One thing was for certain, whatever was about to happen was going to hurt.

She gritted her teeth and, crossing her arms around her body, she pulled out two small canes. As she flicked them expertly, they lengthened, and she stood watching the men in front of her.

Jack laughed. "Oh, so you want to fight first, do you? As you wish. Get her, but don't kill her. I want her to know what's happening to her after you've finished, when it is my turn," he commanded his two men.

As they stepped forward, one moving to the left, the other to the right, Julia did not show a flicker of fear when Jack gave another whistle and there was movement in the trees. She had known there were others keeping watch, but thought they might remain in position for a while at least. This was going to be a short fight, she thought, as she heard movement behind her.

“I warn you now that I do not usually aim to hurt, but tonight is different, so either move out of my way or face the consequences.” Her voice was surprisingly steady as she spoke, watching the men who now circled her.

“Do your worst,” Jack said. “If they cannot beat you, they are no good to me.”

None of his men flinched at the cruel words of their boss; they were too intent on watching Julia. The stalemate was ended seconds later when one in front of her and one of the newcomers at her back both lunged towards her.

Julia released the mechanism of the canes, releasing the blades which shot out at speed from the bottom of the stick; the man in front dropped to the ground, rolling in pain, as did the one unfortunate enough to be at his side. She had aimed directly for the stomach and had scored perfect hits. A second later she was slammed into the body of the man attacking from the rear.

Jabbing her spiked elbows into him as hard as she could, she was able to free herself from his grasp as he jerked back in pain. Her reprieve only lasted a few seconds, but it was enough to start using the cane as a sword while she released a knife from her bodice.

She might struggle to live with herself later if she did any serious damage, but for now this was a fight for her life, and she had to rely on everything she had been taught over the last few months.

Using her weapons, elbows and knees, she was putting up a good fight, but only the two men she had injured at the start remained out of the fight. There had been three more in the woods and they were gaining the upper hand. Julia was tiring quickly, she had never fought as hard or for as long, and she could hear the ringing in her ears as she struggled for breath. But still the punches to her body came whenever they could get close enough.

All three were bleeding, but she could not incapacitate them enough for them to stop. Eventually she was grabbed from behind, her arms pinned to her sides, so she could not use the spikes against her attacker. Gasping for breath, she flung her head back hard and was satisfied to hear a crunch as it made contact with her attacker's nose. He let out a howl of pain but held fast.

"Enough of this!" Jack shouted, and walking over to where Julia was being held, he pulled his fist back and slammed it into her face.

Julia slumped forward unconscious before being dropped on the ground by the thug trying to stem the flow of blood from his nose.

"Pick her up," Jack ordered. "I am going to make her pay for this. Then I will send her home in pieces."

“Do not let any of them escape!” came the cry from the trees as Hugh burst through the undergrowth alongside the footmen and John.

A fresh fight broke out, but this one was over quickly. Jack’s men were injured and tired, certainly not capable of fighting two to one with people intent on winning at any cost. One tried to escape but was shot by John.

“I want them to hang!” Hugh hissed as he battled with Jack. “Do not kill them.”

“There is no need for concern, my friend,” John shouted back at Hugh. “I have only grazed him. I thought you would want to see justice done, as do I.”

Hugh could not allow himself to look at Julia’s prone body or he would falter. Instead, he used the anger inside him to drive home punch after punch to Jack; although Jack was no pushover, he was giving as good as he got.

Wary that the last time they had met he had been stabbed by one of Jack’s men, Hugh ducked and dodged every which way, trying to bring the fight to a close. When everyone else was apprehended, Hugh grinned at Jack. “It is over.”

“Only when I take you down,” Jack said and lunged forward.

Prepared for the move, Hugh knocked Jack’s hand away and landed a punch that Gentleman Jackson would have been proud of. Jack seemed surprised at the move and almost stayed stationary in mid-air before crumpling to the ground.

Hugh bent over, rubbing his hands. “Damn, that hurt,” he said before kneeling next to Julia on the ground. “Julia, can you hear me?”

“Does she breathe?” John asked, moving to Hugh’s side.

Hugh crouched closer to Julia’s face. “Barely,” he said.

“We need a doctor and a magistrate at Half Moon Street, urgently,” John commanded two of the footmen. “Everyone else, get hold of a prisoner, and even if you have to drag them, we are getting out of this park. Hugh, I will help you carry her.”

“No. I can manage,” Hugh said. “You make sure Jack does not get away. I will see him swing for this.”

“We will celebrate when that happens,” John said.

“From what Florence has said, half of London will probably join us.”

***

Julia tried to open her eyes, but only one would co-operate. Blinking the one eye, she looked around her bedchamber. It seemed she had an audience. Hugh, Florence and William all sat at various points around her bed, watching her.

Feeling a strange constriction around her head, she tried to speak. "Ith, hurths," she muttered.

"I am sure it does hurt," Hugh said. "One would say, if one was being harsh, that you deserve to hurt, embarking on such a foolhardy, irresponsible action alone."

Julia did not need to be told how angry Hugh was and she completely understood his sentiments. "Hadth to get to Florenceth," she said.

"Shhussh," William cautioned. "The doctor said it is important that you do not try to speak, or your jaw might be permanently affected."

Julia felt for the bandage, which went around her head and underneath her jaw. It was secured tightly; no wonder she was struggling to speak. Touching her face, she winced at the swelling on her left side. She remembered the punch, now she could feel the damage.

She was about to speak again when her chamber door opened and Grace walked in. "I thought I told you to tell me when she awoke," Grace said to the three of them.

"She's only just opened her eyes, and Uncle Hugh has been cursing at her since," Florence said.

"You are not too old or grand to avoid getting a box around the ears, my lord," Grace said to Hugh. "She needs complete rest and no talking," she looked pointedly at Julia. “You can argue your case when you are recovered, until then you can do as you are told.”

“That will be a first,” Hugh said.

“Enough of that. You have seen her awake, now the three of you can go and leave her be,” Grace instructed. None of them looked like they wanted to move, but when she folded her arms and glared at them, they all reluctantly stood.

“We will be talking about this as soon as you are able,” Hugh said, but kissed her on the head gently and touched her uninjured cheek. “I thought I had lost you; these have been the worst days of my life,” he said quietly before moving away.

William said his goodbye with a kiss and assured her that everything was well and there was nothing to worry about. “Although I must confess that Lord Weston and I have burned your shadow clothing.” Julia’s one eye widened. “It is over,” William continued. “Neither of us could go through this again.”

Julia sighed but nodded her understanding.

Finally, Florençe approached. “I want to throw my arms around you and squeeze but from what the doctor said you are battered and bruised all over,” she said. “I have no idea how I can every repay you, but I promise that I will.”

Julia shook her head slightly, reached out her hand and squeezed Florence’s. “No neeth,” she whispered.

"Right, no more!" Grace said. "Out. The lot of you!"

Julia gave a lopsided smile as they did as they were bid, but she stopped smiling when Grace looked at her.

"Oh, you are in for the scolding of your life when you are well enough, missy," Grace said. "I am convinced you have aged me ten years these last few days. Fortunately for you, you lived, or there would be real trouble."

Julia smiled again and Grace sat down next to her, holding her hand. "If ever you doubted that Lord Weston was madly in love with you, I can assure you that over the last few days that boy has been nearly out of his mind with worry. I honestly believe he would have followed you to the grave if you had not survived, I was really worried about him."

Julia closed her eye, upset that Hugh and the others had been through so much. She could not explain to them her reasoning, but she knew it had been her final act one way or another. The shadow was retired, permanently. She could do no more, and for some reason the urge was no longer there. Instead, the thought of children and a future had started to fill her mind, not how she had to pay a penance for her parents being out that evening at her instigation.

Perhaps Uncle William was right; she could not have altered the course of events at all.

Closing her eyes again, she fell back asleep, dreaming of happy times when her parents had been alive. She knew they would have welcomed Hugh into the family, and with that thought, she was able to sleep soundly.

Chapter 23

Three years later

"I think you should start another club," Florence said to Julia as she walked into the morning room.

"Oh yes? And what would that be?" Julia asked with a smile.

"The happily married club, of course," Florence responded.

"But you are not married. Yet."

"I do not intend ever marrying," Florence answered.

"That has been said by many and we have all succumbed to it," Hugh said, following Florence into the room, carrying a wriggling bundle in his arms. "Freddy wanted to see his mama," he said as he put the baby on the floor, who started to walk on very unsteady feet towards Julia.

"Who is a clever boy?" Julia asked, arms open, ready to receive the baby.

"I do not need to get married now you have an heir," Florence said to Hugh.

Hugh grinned at his wife. "We might have two by Christmas."

"You are increasing again? Oh lovely!" Florence immediately ran to Julia and Freddy and embraced them both.

Julia laughed. "It was supposed to be a secret for a little while longer," she admonished Hugh. "But as usual he has to tell everyone."

"That is because I cannot believe how lucky I am and that my wife keeps bestowing these wonderful children on me," Hugh said, crossing the room and kissing Julia before lifting Freddy up once more and swinging him in the air.

"Eww, could you please wait until I am out of the room?" Florence grimaced.

"Afraid it might be catching?" Hugh teased.

"Not at all," Florence huffed.

"Leave her be," Julia chastised. "You did not like it when you were teased about needing to marry. John has told me all about it."

"He is supposed to be my friend," Hugh grumbled. "He is far too keen to divulge everything to you."

"You are surrounded by the Bluestockings who are equally keen to divulge all my secrets. Isn't it funny how all of the club have completely different lives now? Who would have thought that we had accepted our place in life and then everything has been turned upside down? They still should not tell you my secrets, though; that is unfair."

"And your uncle divulges quite a few things too."

Julia smiled. "Yes, who knew that Uncle William would become your biggest advocate?"

"He still prefers me," Florence said.

"That is because you are as good an inventor as he ever was," Julia said.

"On that note, I had better go and see him. Is he in the garden?"

"Yes, but do not encourage him to start rambling on about a larger building," Julia cautioned. "The space he has is quite enough for his needs."

"I think you are cruel." Florence smiled before leaving the room.

"He would have the whole garden turned into a workshop if we allowed it," Julia said.

"No doubt he will encourage every child we have to be the same as Florence."

"I doubt it, Florence has a natural aptitude to create moving objects."

"I should be thankful, I suppose, that they are no longer making weapons," Hugh drawled.

"Yes, those days are behind them." Julia moved and sat on Hugh's knee while he balanced Freddy on the other knee. "Am I allowed to admit how happy I am?"

Hugh smiled at her. "Only if it is purely of my doing."

"I was thinking last night of the scolding you gave me after the tussle with that man," Julia started.

"Tussle? It was a battering!"

"I am not sure which was worse, the fight or the scolding," Julia continued.

"How can you say that?" Hugh asked incredulously. "I seem to recall that I had barely started before a hussy of a woman began to kiss me senseless. When she had finished, I could barely remember my name let alone what I wanted to scold you about."

Julia smiled. "That is the bit that I like to remember."

"It was that which forced us to get a special licence," Hugh said. "You were very bad."

"I had been through something that made me realise what was important, and waiting to be married was not one of them. I wanted to be with you."

"And I have wanted you every day since. Let me take Freddy back to the nursery, and then I think we should see if we can remember just how good those kisses were," Hugh said, giving Julia a lingering kiss before lifting her and Freddy to stand up.

Julia smiled at him. "That is a fine idea, my lord."

"I am full of them."

"You do have one or two moments of genius, but you have to be given a little push now and again."

Hugh laughed. "With you by my side, I know that is something I am guaranteed to experience. I knew marrying an intelligent woman would be a hardship."

"Not everyone is as lucky as you," Julia said. "I keep you on your toes."

"You do just that. As for the rest of them, they have no idea what they are missing," Hugh said, kissing her fully on the lips. "I just thank my lucky stars that I got to you first."

"I love your flowery speeches," Julia teased.

"Whenever you are around, I cannot seem to do anything else. I am a smitten fool."

"Long may it continue."

"That I can guarantee, my love, even when we are old and grey, with ten children running around our feet."

"Ten children?"

"Maybe five then, but one thing is certain, I will adore you then as much as I do today."

"And I you," Julia said and knew life was more perfect than she could ever have imagined.

The End

Read the next Bluestocking story:- The Bluestocking's Fortune

About the Author

I have had the fortune to live a dream. I've always wanted to write, but life got in the way as it so often does until a few years ago. Then a change in circumstance enabled me to do what I loved: sit down to write. Now writing has taken over my life, holidays being based around research, so much so that no matter where we go, my long-suffering husband says, 'And what connection to the Regency period has this building/town/garden got?'

That dream became a little more surreal when in 2018, I became an Amazon StorytellerUK Finalist with Lord Livesey's Bluestocking. A Regency Romance in the top five of an all-genre competition! It was a truly wonderful experience, I didn't expect to win, but I had a ball at the awards ceremony.

I do appreciate it when readers get in touch, especially if they love the characters as much as I do. Those first few weeks after release is a trying time; I desperately want everyone to love my characters that take months and months of work to bring to life.

If you enjoy the books please would you take the time to write a review on Amazon? Reviews are vital for an author who is just starting out, although I admit to bad ones being crushing. Selfishly I want readers to love my stories!

I can be contacted for any comments you may have, via my website:

www.audreyharrison.co.uk

or

www.facebook.com/AudreyHarrisonAuthor

Please sign-up for email/newsletter – only sent out when there is something to say!

www.audreyharrison.co.uk

You'll receive a free copy of The Unwilling Earl in mobi/epub format for signing-up as a thank you!

Novels by Audrey Harrison

Regency Romances – newest release first

The Captain's Spinster – The Spinster Series – book 1
https://www.amazon.com/dp/B096BDHXBF
https://www.amazon.co.uk/dp/B096BDHXBF
The Spinster's Second Chance – The Spinster Series – book 2
https://www.amazon.com/dp/B09671D13F
https://www.amazon.co.uk/dp/B09671D13F
The American Spinster – The Spinster Series – book 3
https://www.amazon.com/dp/B09LHQ13N4
https://www.amazon.co.uk/dp/B09LHQ13N4
The Colonel's Spinster
https://www.amazon.com/dp/B08N1K9Y4H
https://www.amazon.co.uk/dp/B08N1K9Y4H
Lady Edith's Lonely Heart – The Lonely Hearts Series – book 1
https://www.amazon.com/dp/B0852RMGJJ
https://www.amazon.co.uk/dp/B0852RMGJJ

Miss King's Rescue – The Lonely Hearts Series – book 2

https://www.amazon.com/dp/B08778RJQP

https://www.amazon.co.uk/dp/B08778RJQP

Captain Jones's Temptation – The Lonely Hearts Series – book 3

https://www.amazon.com/dp/B08775663R

https://www.amazon.co.uk/dp/B08775663R

The Lonely Lord

https://www.amazon.com/dp/B07S1X5NBZ

https://www.amazon.co.uk/dp/B07S1X5NBZ

The Drummond Series:-

Lady Lou the Highwayman – Drummond series Book 1

https://www.amazon.com/dp/B07NDX3HV2

https://www.amazon.co.uk/dp/B07NDX3HV2

Saving Captain Drummond – Drummond Series Book 2

https://www.amazon.com/dp/B07NFBRZFG

https://www.amazon.co.uk/dp/B07NFBRZFG

Book bundle – The Drummonds

https://www.amazon.com/dp/B08TVYYBZY

https://www.amazon.co.uk/dp/B08TVYYBZY

Lord Livesey's Bluestocking (Amazon Storyteller Finalist 2018)

https://www.amazon.com/dp/B07D3T6L93

https://www.amazon.co.uk/dp/B07D3T6L93

Return to the Regency – A Regency Time-travel novel

https://www.amazon.com/dp/B078C87HVX

https://www.amazon.co.uk/dp/B078C87HVX

My Foundlings:-

The Foundling Duke – The Foundlings Book 1

https://www.amazon.com/dp/B071KTT9CD

https://www.amazon.co.uk/dp/B071KTT9CD

The Foundling Lady – The Foundlings Book 2

https://www.amazon.com/dp/B072L2D7PF

https://www.amazon.co.uk/dp/B072L2D7PF

Book bundle – The Foundlings

https://www.amazon.com/dp/B07Q6YLND4

https://www.amazon.co.uk/dp/B07Q6YLND4

Mr Bailey's Lady

https://www.amazon.com/dp/B01NACMFVJ

https://www.amazon.co.uk/dp/B01NACMFVJ

The Spy Series:-

My Lord the Spy

https://www.amazon.com/dp/B01F11ZRM8

https://www.amazon.co.uk/dp/B01F11ZRM8

My Earl the Spy

https://www.amazon.com/dp/B01F12NG8E

https://www.amazon.co.uk/dp/B01F12NG8E

Book bundle – The Spying Lords

https://www.amazon.com/dp/B07RV3JQFP

https://www.amazon.co.uk/dp/B07RV3JQFP

The Captain's Wallflower

https://www.amazon.com/dp/B018PDBGLK

https://www.amazon.co.uk/dp/B018PDBGLK

The Four Sisters' Series:-

Rosalind – Book 1

https://www.amazon.com/dp/B00WWTXSA6
https://www.amazon.co.uk/dp/B00WWTXSA6

Annabelle – Book 2
https://www.amazon.com/dp/B00WWTXRWA
https://www.amazon.co.uk/dp/B00WWTXRWA

Grace – Book 3
https://www.amazon.com/dp/B00WWUBEWO
https://www.amazon.co.uk/dp/B00WWUBEWO

Eleanor – Book 4
https://www.amazon.com/dp/B00WWUBF1E
https://www.amazon.co.uk/dp/B00WWUBF1E

Book Bundle – The Four Sisters
https://www.amazon.com/dp/B01416W0C4
https://www.amazon.co.uk/dp/B01416W0C4

The Inconvenient Trilogy:-

The Inconvenient Ward – Book 1
https://www.amazon.com/dp/B00KCJUJFA
https://www.amazon.co.uk/dp/B00KCJUJFA

The Inconvenient Wife – Book 2
https://www.amazon.com/dp/B00KCJVQU2
https://www.amazon.co.uk/dp/B00KCJVQU2

The Inconvenient Companion – Book 3
https://www.amazon.com/dp/B00KCK87T4
https://www.amazon.co.uk/dp/B00KCK87T4

Book bundle – An Inconvenient Trilogy
https://www.amazon.com/dp/B00PHQIZ18
https://www.amazon.co.uk/dp/B00PHQIZ18

The Complicated Earl
https://www.amazon.com/dp/B00BCN90DC
https://www.amazon.co.uk/dp/B00BCN90DC

The Unwilling Earl (Novella)
https://www.amazon.com/dp/B00BCNE2HG
https://www.amazon.co.uk/dp/B00BCNE2HG

Other Eras
A Very Modern Lord
Years Apart

Printed in Great Britain
by Amazon

49431755R00146